KINGDOM
OF THE DEEP

E.J. ALTBACKER

PUFFIN

PUFFIN BOOKS

Published by the Penguin Group
Penguin Books Ltd, 80 Strand, London WC2R 0RL, England
Penguin Group (USA) Inc., 375 Hudson Street, New York, New York 10014, USA
Penguin Group (Canada), 90 Eglinton Avenue East, Suite 700, Toronto, Ontario, Canada M4P 2Y3
(a division of Pearson Penguin Canada Inc.)
Penguin Ireland, 25 St Stephen's Green, Dublin 2, Ireland (a division of Penguin Books Ltd)
Penguin Group (Australia), 707 Collins Street, Melbourne, Victoria 3008, Australia
(a division of Pearson Australia Group Pty Ltd)
Penguin Books India Pvt Ltd, 11 Community Centre, Panchsheel Park, New Delhi – 110 017, India
Penguin Group (NZ), 67 Apollo Drive, Rosedale, Auckland 0632, New Zealand
(a division of Pearson New Zealand Ltd)
Penguin Books (South Africa) (Pty) Ltd, Block D, Rosebank Office Park, 181 Jan Smuts Avenue,
Parktown North, Gauteng 2193, South Africa

Penguin Books Ltd, Registered Offices: 80 Strand, London WC2R 0RL, England

puffinbooks.com

First published in USA in Razorbill, an imprint of Penguin Books Ltd, 2012
Published in Great Britain in Puffin Books 2012
001

The moral right of the author and illustrator has been asserted

Printed in Great Britain by Clays Ltd, St Ives plc

British Library Cataloguing in Publication Data
A CIP catalogue record for this book is available from the British Library

ISBN: 978-0-141-34000-5

www.greenpenguin.co.uk

MIX
Paper from
responsible sources
FSC
www.fsc.org   FSC™ C018179

Penguin Books is committed to a sustainable
future for our business, our readers and our planet.
This book is made from Forest Stewardship
Council™ certified paper.

ALWAYS LEARNING   **PEARSON**

PUFFIN BOOKS

KINGDOM
OF THE DEEP

The Shark Wars series

For Mom and Dad

THIRTEEN YEARS AGO

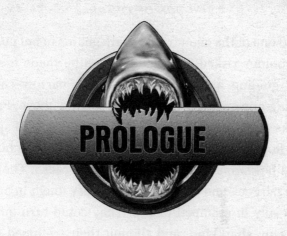

PROLOGUE

"QUICKLY, MY SON!" GRAYNOLDUS SHOUTED AT his terrified pup. "You must swim like you have never swum before!" The little megalodon wasn't old enough to speak but understood and churned his tail as fast as he could. Would it be enough?

Graynoldus could not believe how the situation had spun out of control so quickly and completely. It was madness!

Did Kaleth know of the coup by Drinnok? Drinnok was a bully and a loudmouth, but Graynoldus never would have thought that the giant mako shark would send King Bollagan and his Line to the Sparkle Blue! And were Hokuu and the mako *fin'jaa* that agreed with Drinnok part of this conspiracy? If so, Kaleth was in terrible danger! Graynoldus had to get to the other side and warn the rest. Everything depended on it!

"Stop him! By the order of Drinnok, stop him now!"

yelled one of the giant frilled shark guards in hot pursuit. Graynoldus risked a glance back as he made a sharp turn, guiding his young son into the narrow canyon leading upwards towards the new world above. Frilled sharks were better suited to swimming in tight spaces and flowed over the jagged ridges and switchbacks while he scraped himself on the sharp rocks. The frills were part eel, and that made them very tough in a fight, especially in cramped places. They could turn quicker than any sharkkind, and though their tri-tipped teeth were small compared to those of a megalodon, they could tear chunks off a shark with alarming efficiency. Frills also had a razor-sharp spike on the end of their tails that could pierce even the toughest shark hide. And they were swimming in a swarm of at least twenty.

If he and his pup were caught...

Graynoldus kept his attention on moving upwards through the twisting passage. There was no time for playing "what if" right now. He would deal with that situation if the time came. Graynoldus ground his teeth and bore down, pushing his son forward.

Fifth Shiver had been sealed off for aeons. It had been so long that only in legend was it whispered that there were a sun and moon above what was called the *chop-chop*, a term that had lost all meaning. Their watery world was hemmed in by a limestone and lumo-encrusted boundary. You could swim five thousand aqualeagues in any direction and no further. Such had it been since long after the time of Tyro, the First Fish, who had created all sharkkind and then set them in a Line to protect those who lived in the ocean. There were ancient stories that the Big Blue was bigger than their own waters, but there was no way to prove it.

Not until the seaquake.

The titanic quake had cracked the stone barrier imprisoning them all and opened a path upwards into the wider ocean world. A scout had swum through the falling rocks, hissing steams and glowing lava and made it to the other side! What he discovered was hailed as a miracle, a sign that their time was not over in the Big Blue. Graynoldus, too, was overjoyed when he swam out from the warm darkness of their pocket ocean. It had taken some time for his eyes to adjust, but he had seen the waters of the Big Blue along with the sun and moon above! Miraculous!

It was called the chop-chop because it was *choppy* from the waves! Who knew?

But this was a different world. It was much colder, the water tasted different, and most importantly it was teeming with brand-new sharkkind and dwellers. They were younger races but doing wonderfully.

Their wise king, Bollagan, had decided that other than Kaleth, who was fifth in his Line, and a small group to guide the younger race of sharkkind, no one would swim into the new world until he'd had time to think over the consequences. Rightly, Bollagan thought that the younger races should swim their own current, with just a little help from their older, wiser cousins as in the ancient times. He did not want to start a war by rushing out and surprising them. If Fifth Shiver was to join the new world, they should live in peace with the younger races.

Although Bollagan was supported by Graynoldus and most others of his Line, Drinnok disagreed. He thought that they, the *prehistores*, as the younger race called them, had the right to reclaim the Big Blue as their own.

"If they have a problem with that, then they will die!" he had shouted at the council meeting last night. Sure, it was a disagreement, but Drinnok was a disagreeable fin and argued at most of the council meetings. Then Graynoldus had awoken to the sounds of battle this morning and word that the king and the rest of the Line were dead. Now Graynoldus was the only one left to tell Kaleth of Drinnok's treachery! With Kaleth at his side, perhaps they would be able to deal with Drinnok before he could invade the Big Blue.

If she was still alive.

Graynoldus used his massive tail to dislodge the loose rocks he hurtled past, but it wasn't enough. The frilled sharks, willing allies in Drinnok's plan, were too agile. A pocket of steam blasted out, scalding his side. The path was swelling and contracting, as if it hadn't yet decided if it wanted to stay open.

"Swim, my boy! Swim!" Graynoldus urged his son

as he felt a tug on his tail. One of the frilled sharks had taken a bite from it. Their teeth were so sharp you almost didn't know you were being bitten.

Almost.

Graynoldus pushed little Gray forward and then flipped over, blasting the attacker away with his massive tail. The rest of the frills came forward in a rush. Each time one of the swarm struck, a scoop of flesh was taken from his flank or tail. Graynoldus was streaming so much blood that little Gray had stopped in shock, his mouth trembling. His son watched as Graynoldus was eaten alive.

They weren't going to make it ...

"Swim, Gray! Swim or you will be punished! Do what I say!"

Little Gray, frightened beyond belief, began moving upwards once more.

Graynoldus turned and brought his own massive dagger teeth to bear, snapping two frills clean in half. They went writhing and twisting into the blackness. He ground several others to jelly against the rough passageway before turning to his enemies. The way was narrow enough that the frills had to attack him face-to-face. Though Graynoldus dwarfed any one of them, the combined strength of the swarm would tear him apart.

"You will not pass!" he yelled with all his strength. "By Bollagan's mighty heart, YOU WILL NOT PASS!"

Then the mountainous walls around him cracked

and heaved. An orange glow brightened the waters before deepening to an angry red.

Steam hissed, louder and louder.

Graynoldus turned and looked at his son for what he knew would be the last time. "Swim, Gray! Swim! I love you!"

Little Gray disappeared around the last corner.

Good boy, Graynoldus thought.

The frilled sharks rushed forward to finish him.

And then the world exploded.

PRESENT
DAY

CHAPTER 1

"AQUA-ZAYDOR?" GRAY REPEATED HALTINGLY TO Kaleth, the megalodon Seazarein, who rested on her throne with a look that was somehow both haughty and annoyed. *Aquasidor*. The strange word was a title that meant messenger or bringer of news, and Gray had just been given both the title and job.

Well, not given. More like ordered.

Barkley and Mari hovered near him, open-mouthed from the surprise of it all. Only Takiza was composed. The betta fish floated as if nothing out of the ordinary was happening.

"Aquasidor! Aquasidor! Pronounce it correctly," Kaleth told him, her eyes flashing. The throne she rested on had actually been fashioned for a prehistore shark – which the Seazarein was, being a megalodon – and even had a hole for her tail.

A megalodon!

This in itself was incredible. Until five minutes ago, when Gray had swum into the cave with Takiza, Barkley and Mari, he hadn't known that any others of his kind existed in the Big Blue. Now, in addition to Kaleth, there were giant prehistores lining each side of the cavern. They weren't megalodons but the ancient, larger versions of blue sharks, hammerheads, bulls and tigers. They were her guards, Gray guessed.

Strangely, there were no makos.

But where did they come from? Were there others apart from the ones here? Gray had so many questions, but it seemed he would have to wait to ask them. The Seazarein and Takiza were perfectly happy having a conversation in front of Gray, Barkley and Mari without including them.

Apparently Kaleth was fifth in the Line for Fifth Shiver, whose king was Bollagan. They were direct descendants of Tyro and First Shiver! It boggled the mind. Kaleth was a young shark – seemingly too young to be in the Line – but apparently where she came from, sharkkind grew up fast, or not at all. She had been holding Bollagan's place here in the Big Blue, but the underwater passageway between her ocean and the Big Blue had closed, leaving her to be the Seazarein. It seemed there had also been some argument between Bollagan and his fourth in the Line, a mako named Drinnok, who apparently wanted to take over the Big Blue. Or worse. It was all so confusing to Gray.

Everything seemed to be a giant jumble of unfamiliar names and places.

"Takiza, how can Graynoldus be trusted to manage any situation I put him in when he can't even *say* Aquasidor correctly?" asked the Seazarein.

That was also odd. Why was Kaleth calling him Graynoldus?

"Hey, he's just heard the word for the first time!" said Barkley, coming to Gray's defence.

Kaleth gave Barkley a look as if he were unworthy to be in the same cavern with her. "Dogfish should be seen and not heard. And *neither* seen *nor* heard would be even better."

Mari bumped Barkley before he could give one of his smart replies, and he ground his teeth instead. Kaleth turned to Takiza. "The question remains: can Graynoldus do the job of keeping the foolish fins in these seas from fighting each other so we can concentrate on the traitor Hokuu and the much larger danger he represents?"

The betta ruffled his colourful and billowy fins as he gave the question some thought. Takiza's fins seemed so delicate, but the Siamese fighting fish, though tiny in size compared to any shark, was a master of shar-kata and the greatest fighter that Gray had ever seen. "He may need some training about the particulars of the position, but his instincts are surprisingly adequate," he told her.

"I have a teacher who swears she can teach any shark

as long as they're not completely stupid." The Seazarein looked pointedly at Gray as if trying to determine if he were completely stupid.

Takiza turned towards Gray also, pausing longer than was necessary before saying, "He is not. Most of the time."

Barkley whispered, "Sweet compliment!"

"Shut your cod hole," Gray hissed, bumping his friend out of his hover for good measure. Mari cleared her throat to warn them, but it was too late. Kaleth and Takiza were watching them both.

"If you've finished *playing*, there are important things to do!" Kaleth thundered.

"Sorry," Gray said, his tail drooping.

Mari swished her long-lobed thresher tail to get Kaleth's attention. "May I speak, Your . . . Majesty?"

"Call me Kaleth," the Seazarein answered. "Titles give you a big head."

"Well, Kaleth, it seems like you're making all these decisions without even asking Gray what he wants to do. I mean, he's the leader of Riptide Shiver and won a battle of life and death against Finnivus and Indi Shiver. Doesn't he deserve to be treated with a little respect?"

The Seazarein straightened and gave Mari a searing gaze but then nodded. "You and your shiver have been through a lot, that's true." She motioned at Gray with a fin. "And your victory in that war is the only reason you are here. I could use some help. The last Aquasidor, a frilled shark by the name of Hokuu, continues to be a problem today, which is why there hasn't been one for over a decade. But now there is too much going on at once and my influence must be felt to keep the peace. No ordinary sharkkind will do. It must be a shark that others will immediately respect."

"I–I don't know if I'm that shark," Gray stuttered.

Kaleth slammed her tail against the ground behind her throne. "Don't put down your accomplishments! You have earned respect, and I need to use it. The danger, should I fail, would be much worse than if you had lost to Finnivus."

Gray gulped. "Worse than Finnivus and Indi Shiver taking over the entire Big Blue?"

The thought was frightening. It was only by the edge of their pointy teeth that a combined force of Riptide, AuzyAuzy, Hammer and Vortex Shivers, along with Tik-Tun and his orcas, had managed to defeat the mad emperor Finnivus and his Black Wave armada in a titanic battle in the depths by the Maw. And now there was something worse in the current? Already?

Takiza flicked his fins in agreement. "It is true. If Hokuu releases Drinnok and his prehistore allies from the under-waters, they have the potential to wipe every shark and dweller from the Big Blue."

"King Bollagan will never allow Drinnok to go that far, but the danger *is* great," Kaleth said.

Takiza gave the Seazarein a head bob before

adding, "We have not heard from Bollagan since the passage closed, which is why it is best to be prepared for anything."

Mari's eyes widened and she asked, "What do you mean *prehistore* allies?"

"And what are the under-waters?" asked Barkley straight after that.

Kaleth stared hard at Barkley and Mari but answered in clipped tones as if they were dumb pups. "The under-waters are where I come from and where many other prehistores live. They are located *under* these waters, hence their name."

"Wow, that was super-snobby and arrogant, but let's move on," said Barkley. "Who's this Hokuu?"

Kaleth's eyes blazed as if she wanted to eat Barkley, but he continued undeterred. "How come I've never heard of him if he's such a giant threat? Everyone in the ocean knew about Finnivus."

"Which was his undoing," Takiza replied. "Hokuu is much smarter. He swims in the shadows, waiting for his time to strike. And, as I have told Gray previously, he was my Shiro, which makes him exceptionally dangerous."

Now Barkley did react. "Hokuu was your master? He trained you to do all that magical stuff that lets you toss sharks around like they were minnows in a whirlpool?"

"Shar-kata is *not* magic," Takiza answered. "It is a form of training that enables one to take power from the ocean itself." The betta frowned. "And Hokuu was much better at it when I was *his* Nulo ages ago."

"That's not good," Mari whispered, but since it was so quiet in the cavern, everyone heard it.

Gray had been Takiza's Nulo, or student, until recently. If the gap between his and Takiza's abilities was any clue, Hokuu would be almost impossible to beat. Add to that prehistores, and Gray felt a tingling fear slide down his spine and settle like a cold rock in his stomach.

"Okay, I'm officially worried," Barkley told Gray.

"No one cares what you think!" shouted Kaleth. "This is important sharkkind business and you are a dog*fish*!"

"They're called dog *sharks*," Mari said, defending Barkley. Why was Kaleth picking on him? Barkley always complained about how dogfish were disrespected by other sharks. Gray usually dismissed it because his friend could whine for no reason at all – as could anyone – from time to time. Sure, Barkley took complaining to a whole different level, but here it seemed that Kaleth didn't think much of him *because* he was a dogfish.

To Gray, that was a mark against her, not Barkley.

Kaleth swished her tail in short, irritated strokes as she balanced on the throne. "Graynoldus, I want a shark to be the teeth of will around the Big Blue as my Aquasidor. I need to keep the peace everywhere else so my guardians can concentrate on finding and stopping Hokuu." Kaleth scowled at Barkley and Mari before either could ask a question. "Since the path between our two seas closed, I have no way of knowing what's happening down below with Drinnok, so I don't know what he's up to exactly. I do know that Hokuu fights me at every turn in the Big Blue and has tried to kill me. If whatever he's planning comes to pass, there will be blood in the water like you've never seen before. So, make your choice. Will you help or not? I can't use a fin who will not fully commit to following my orders."

Barkley was about to open his mouth when Gray slashed his tail through the water. "I guess lounging around in the Riptide homewaters isn't something I get to do right now," he told his friends.

Mari smiled a little half smile. "But you've done so much already, Gray."

"It's true," Barkley agreed. "You deserve some rest and relaxation."

The Seazarein interrupted from the throne. "*Deserve* has absolutely nothing to do with it, dogfish."

Barkley relished ignoring Kaleth, flicking his tail at her. The megalodon leader made a rumbling noise deep in her throat but didn't reply.

Gray faced Kaleth and Takiza. "I'll do it. I'll be your Aquasidor." This time he pronounced the word correctly, earning a nod from Kaleth. Gray glanced at Barkley and Mari. "I just don't trust anyone else to do this. Especially

if it means keeping the peace we fought so hard for."
Barkley and Mari were quiet, but they understood.

Gray looked at Kaleth. "So. When do we start?"

"At once, of course."

CHAPTER 2

VELENKA HOVERED IN THE DARK, A FEW SILVERY streams of moonglow brightening the rock floor of her cell and creating pools of light. This and a few smaller holes through the lava rock provided her with enough current to breathe. Because the blackness was so complete otherwise, it seemed as if the hazy tubes of moonlight were solid, cutting her cramped space into smaller pieces. Even when the sun rose high over the Big Blue, it remained murky in the underwater dungeon where Velenka was locked. Many would be unnerved by the gloom she was forced to endure day after day.

Not Velenka.

She enjoyed the dark, always had. Ever since she was young, she'd preferred hunting at night. When the sun set and the ocean grew dark, it was the time of the predator. And despite her predicament, Velenka was *still* a predator.

This was all Gray's fault, she thought, grinding her needle teeth together. Velenka's teeth itched when she wasn't being honest with herself and that maddening tickle was there again. After all, was her situation really Gray's fault? Some of it, undoubtedly. Yet she had swum a current so thin that no one else would be alive to tell the tale had *they* been forced to do it.

First, when she'd managed to prevent Goblin and his shiver from being overwhelmed by Razor Shiver. Then, she'd tried to turn the stubborn Gray to her will and that had careened out of control. And after that, when Velenka finally took control of Riptide Shiver, Finnivus and his Black Wave armada had come in and ruined everything once more. Time after time, she had been forced to dip her snout to someone more powerful!

You *want* control but never enough to *earn* it, teased a small voice in her mind.

Velenka silently and totally disagreed. *Not true! I deserve it! No one deserves it more than me!* The itching in her gums became maddening as she silently blamed Gray once more. She ground her teeth fiercely until one snapped off with a *tink*.

The sound echoed off the smooth lava rock walls. It was then she heard a noise – several noises, in fact. They echoed down the slender holes in the wall from the Riptide homewaters. There were shouts of "Alarm!" and "Intruder!" Her cell was so quiet, apart from the slow current that kept her alive, that Velenka could hear individual sharkkind tearing this way and that through the water above.

She moved over to the largest of the holes in her cell to take a look. A small escaping bubble of gas had created it before the lava had solidified in the water, so it was still very narrow, even though it was the biggest. Looking almost straight at the moon, Velenka's eyes watered. She forced herself to bear the brightness and gradually, they adjusted. Groups of sharks, probably patrols, were rushing back and forth. The yelling increased.

"I wonder what's got them so spooked?" Velenka whispered in the gloom.

"Me," said a voice behind her.

Velenka was so startled she smashed her snout into her little portal of the Big Blue. She whirled and saw –

Something impossible.

It was a monstrous eel, or perhaps a sea snake – no, it was just too big to be either of those. Velenka remembered a story she'd heard when she was a pup. There was one type of rare sharkkind that had remained the same as their prehistore cousins through the aeons, a living prehistore. They were called frilled sharks and swam the depths of the Deep Blue. That's what this snaky horror was, a frilled shark.

It was hideous. Its large head, which was thicker than her midsection, had a mouth filled with wicked, multi-pointed teeth. Its eyes glittered emerald green even in the darkness of her prison. The monster's body was flatter than a sea snake's, but because of its size, it was taller than she was except towards the end of its tail, which had a wicked spike.

Velenka found herself at the back wall of her tiny cell. With the monster so close the whale-rib bars seemed thin and brittle. For the first and only time Velenka wished her prison was sturdier. Much sturdier.

"My poor girl," the frilled shark said. "You look like you've seen a ghost. But I'm not a ghost, I'm your saviour. I am Hokuu."

"Nice to meet you," Velenka managed. Hokuu laughed, the sound echoing off the lava rock.

"So, how have you been?" Hokuu asked. Velenka's eyes, already very large, widened a bit more. She hovered there, mouth open, not knowing what to say. "This place. It isn't very nice, is it?" he continued.

"No, it's not," she replied.

"But that's the way of it for you in this world, and makos in general, don't you think?" Hokuu asked, his emerald eyes boring into her. "I've found that makos are very smart. But other sharkkind, they call it deviousness. Like being smart is a bad thing."

Velenka felt as if a trap was closing but nodded. Makos were always distrusted. It was rare for them to be chosen as leaders of mixed shivers. And everyone thought they were sneaky. "I agree, of course, but may I ask what you want from me?"

"Polite and smart. Excellent. I heard that about you."

The frilled shark poked his spiked tail through the bars and tapped Velenka between the eyes. The tip was razor sharp and she had no doubt it would go right through her skull if Hokuu wished. "I want you to join me."

Velenka's insides turned to ice, but she didn't know why. This was an opportunity, a chance to get out of her tiny cell. So why was she afraid? She pushed the feeling aside. "Let's go," she told him.

"Not today," he answered. "It's better that you stay here where I can find you for now. Don't worry, I'll be back. When I do come, be prepared to serve me. And for that service you will be rewarded like no other shark in this Big Blue."

The part about being rewarded was appealing, but Velenka found herself thinking that she'd never work for anyone again unless it suited her goals. Hokuu seemed to know this and smiled. "These sharks will question you about the deaths that happened tonight," the frilled shark hissed. "When they do, find out what you can about the Seazarein."

"I will. I promise. But –"

Hokuu cut her off with a rippling shake of his long tail. "You don't even know what a Seazarein is, do you?"

"Only the legend. They haven't swum the Big Blue for millions of years."

Hokuu smiled. "You're not up on current events. The Seazarein is back. She's real and wants to keep the oceans for herself. But they're not hers! Or any of the puny shivers here that claim pieces of them as their own. Anyway, when the time is right, I'll give you your freedom."

"Yes!" Velenka said. "I'll do what you want. Thank you."

Hokuu smirked but said nothing. Then he was gone as if he had never been there. Velenka let out a ragged sigh, more nervous than she should be. Sure, she didn't know anything about Hokuu or his plans for her, but this was a chance to better her situation. How could that be a bad thing?

CHAPTER 3

IN A RARE BREAK BETWEEN HIS NEW LESSONS, Gray hovered in the towering gold-greenie, which floated more than sixty metres off the ocean floor. The field was immense, larger than he had ever seen. Gold-greenie was rare, and to see so much of it, and growing so big, was amazing. This was part of the Seazarein's homewaters, which Gray now knew were called Fathomir after a great leader of Second Shiver. It also hid the strong point of Kaleth's territory, the cavern where her throne was. Outside the entrance to this cavern lay the ruins of a landshark city with columns of granite, some of which were still standing. The throne cavern itself was well protected, and just twenty finja could hold off an armada from inside.

But her *guardians*, as the Seazarein called the finja, were always hyper-alert and on the lookout for Hokuu. Gray would have liked to know more about the dangerous frilled shark, but neither Takiza nor Kaleth would tell him anything.

Gray and Barkley had caught their lunch in the incredibly fish-filled gold-greenie of Fathomir. Barkley, with his ghostfin training, was a much better hunter than he had been even a year ago, and both had fed well. Afterwards, their lunch break had turned into a game. Gray supposed it could be called a drill – especially if they were caught – but it was more fun than anything. And he needed some fun. Mari, along with the others who had come with him, had already left for Riptide to tell Striiker what was happening and that he would need to lead. Gray hoped the big great white would do a good job. As it was, he was kept far too busy to even consider swimming home.

There were so many lessons Gray thought his head would explode: lessons on how to speak, lessons about protocol, lessons on previous Aquasidors and their missions along with the mistakes they made, lessons on history, lessons on how to greet kings, queens, princes and princesses, lessons on how to react when you received a compliment or a gift – lessons about everything. Gray wouldn't have been surprised if there'd been a lesson about the correct way to clear his throat. It was a relief to clear his mind, even for a little while.

Barkley had challenged him to a best-of-five match in one-to-one combat after they'd eaten. Of course, he had issued the challenge when they were deep in the gold kelp field. Barkley wasn't dumb. Even with his ghostfin skills, a dogfish didn't stand a sardine's chance against Gray in open water. Gray was much larger and stronger.

In the greenie, though, Barkley was as sneaky as a sea spider, and right now they were tied, two all. Both of Barkley's strikes had come after Gray had wandered into an area where his friend had hidden himself perfectly. Some of the gold-greenie stalks were so thick and leafy that a single strand could hide Barkley completely. While most fins would try a successful tactic again and again until it was defeated, Gray felt that his friend would do the opposite.

But maybe he's expecting me to think that, Gray thought. After all, he is sneaky.

He reached out with his senses as Takiza had taught him. Well, was *trying* to teach him. Gray couldn't do it every time. But when he was calm and there was no pressure, sometimes his senses acted like the sonar the dolphins used but without all the clicking. In addition to a shark's lateral line, which detected vibrations, Takiza had taught Gray about these things called ampullae, which could sense the electric fields that all living things generated.

Gray had asked if Takiza was "ampullae-ing my tail", which the betta didn't find funny at all. These sensors were real, but it took practice for them to be more than a very short-range thing. Gray closed his eyes. This seemed to help somehow, but Takiza always got mad when he did it. "Use *all* your senses, not one less than all!" he would huff.

Gray glided carefully through the gigantic greenie field. He could feel the tide moving the thick kelp back and forth. He felt hundreds of fish swimming around, looking for their own meals. Gray dismissed their smaller *shadows*, as he thought of the electrical signals, as background noise. They were too little to be Barkley. He felt several larger sharkkind in the area, the Seazarein's guardians. Those were too big.

Then Gray felt something that caught his attention, so he focused. It was behind and above him, hidden inside a thick patch of greenie, moving with the tide. That was sly, to move with the kelp as the tides pushed it.

Gotcha, Gray thought.

Barkley was almost invisible.

Almost ...

Gray allowed himself to drift near the patch of greenie, making his naked dorsal fin an inviting target. He felt Barkley burst forward from the kelp, though his friend didn't make a sound swimming. Before the dogfish could get close, Gray cut a circular turn up and then back down.

Gray had him bang to rights and Barkley knew it. "That's impossible!" He scowled, not even attempting to defend himself. "Have you grown eyes in the back of your head?"

Gray nudged the dogfish in the flank with his snout. "And that's game!"

"If you have quite finished fooling around, it's time

for your next lesson." Takiza floated between the two, looking at them crossly.

"Oh, this wasn't a game, Shiro," Gray told him as seriously as he could. "We were training. I was practising one of your lessons – you know, the one about –"

Takiza chopped his colourful, gauzy fins through the water. "It so happens that in my own youth I *invented* the excuse of saying I was training when caught playing. It did not work for me then, and it certainly will not work for you now since – as I said – I invented that excuse." Takiza looked over at Barkley. "And if you want to hide undetected in the greenie, you must be more like greenie."

"That doesn't make any sense," Barkley whispered to Gray as Takiza motioned them towards the Seazarein's cavern.

Join the club, thought Gray. Every other thing he was told these days didn't make sense.

"And so, Aquasidor Surex did what, exactly, wrong?" asked Judijoan. Judijoan was Gray's history, manners and protocol teacher and also the Seazarein's advisor. She was an ancient oarfish. Her slender silvery body shone in the throne cavern, and she had crimson fins with a plume of the same colour arching from her forehead. She was at least as long as Gray and had a kind face, although the longer he took to answer, the more sour her expression became.

Barkley gave Gray a silent fin motion to say something – anything.

"What ... Aquasidor Surex ... did ... wrong ... was wrong...really, really, wrong..."

Takiza rolled his eyes as Gray stretched out the time so he could think of an answer. He had absolutely no idea.

"Yes, that much was established by telling you a story called 'The Short and Sad Term of Aquasidor Surex'." Judijoan had a disconcerting habit of rising to hold herself straight up and down so she towered over him as she scowled. The oarfish sighed and glanced at the Seazarein. She continued, "He made *many* mistakes. But in this case, what did Surex do to start the cascade of events that ultimately led to his own death?"

"Aquasidor Surex ... made many, many ... so many ... mistakes ..."

Takiza shook his fins back and forth. "I can take no more!"

"I'm sorry, I don't know!" Gray said. "I'm trying, but the story went on for two hours. I have no idea why Goshen Shiver decided to send Aquasidor Surex to the Sparkle Blue unless he told them a story as long as the one I just heard!"

"Of course you do! He made the same mistake you always do!" Takiza snorted. "Think!"

Gray tried, but nothing came into his mind because

he made mistakes all day. It seemed like he made a mistake every time he opened his mouth.

Wait! That was it!

Gray looked at Judijoan and answered, "He should have remained silent because he didn't know the answer, but instead he guessed. Aquasidor Surex's main mistake was having no idea and saying something that was completely wrong."

"Well done!" the oarfish said. "That was a difficult one."

"Compared to what?" the Seazarein asked. "If Graynoldus doesn't know what I need him to say or *not* say when I need him to say or *not* say it, he'll do more harm than good." Kaleth turned to Takiza. "What do you think?"

The betta hovered, swishing his gauzy fins before answering. "He is not as slow as he seems to be at this precise moment."

Kaleth nodded. "Gray, I know everything is crashing on to you at once, and I am sorry. But there are things happening around this Big Blue that I'm dealing with apart from this. If there were any other way, believe me, I would explore those options. I need you to try harder. The orcas and Hideg Shiver are near war because of an ancient dispute and that needs to be stopped."

"I have heard that their leader, Palink, can be fairly chowderheaded on most days," Takiza remarked.

The Seazarein swished her massive tail. "Apparently so. He wants to pick a fight with Tik-Tun and his orca battle pods. And meanwhile, suddenly AuzyAuzy and Hammer Shivers are also in dispute."

Gray looked at Barkley. They were both shocked. Tik-Tun was ready to go to war? And AuzyAuzy and Hammer were fighting each other? All three had been allies against Finnivus and his Black Wave armada barely a month ago! How could this be?

Before Gray or Barkley could ask anything, the oarfish swished her slender body and used her tail to point at him. "Let's proceed with a speed round."

"Right," Gray answered. "Let's do this."

"What was the fifteenth Seazarein's name?" Judijoan asked.

"Um, don't tell me, I know this one – Johnny ... big ... tail?"

"Johannes Longflanks," Barkley said.

The Seazarein slapped her massive tail against the wall before either Takiza or Judijoan could reprimand Barkley. "Quiet! No helping, especially from you!"

"What does that mean?" asked the dogfish.

"Silence!" Takiza told him. Barkley closed his mouth with an audible click.

Judijoan cracked her tail into Gray's flank to get his attention as she asked another question. "In order of distance away from the continent, which shivers are closest to the prime meridian underneath the African land mass?"

Gray twitched his fins up and down. "Let's see,

Kelpengreenie Shiver, Deep Rush and then, um ...
Barkley?"

"Corallis."

"Silence!" yelled the Seazarein.

"But if I know the answers, I can help Gray."

The Seazarein slammed her tail against the throne.
"No, you won't! I can't have a dogfish solving problems
when my Aquasidor meets the other ancient shivers for
the first time as my Aquasidor. It's ridiculous!"

Barkley looked at the Seazarein, genuinely
perplexed. "How is that ridiculous?"

Kaleth didn't seem to understand Barkley's
confusion. She answered, "Because you're a dogfish.
You're not even sharkkind."

"Oh, really?" Barkley huffed.

"Yes, really," the Seazarein said with disdain. "Look
at you."

Barkley was so shocked he didn't say anything. Gray
couldn't let this drift off, though. "Kaleth, Barkley has
been extremely helpful to me and Riptide Shiver and –"

"Silence!" shouted Takiza, cutting Gray off. "You
dare correct the Seazarein?"

"I'm not correcting her!"

Barkley tried to get a word in. "You're blaming this
on Gray?"

Before either could say anything else, Takiza swept
them out of the room. "I believe it's time for you two to
take a swim," the betta ordered.

Once they were out of the audience chamber, Takiza stared first at Barkley and then at Gray. It was one of those long and imperious stares he was so good at. "I understand that Kaleth's manners can be off-putting, but she is not from here and has much on her mind. You cannot take any of it personally. Neither of you." And without another word, the betta left.

"That could have gone better," Gray said.

"What's up with her, though?" asked Barkley. "Did you hear what she said to me?"

Gray gave his friend a nudge on the flank, trying to cheer him up. "Look, Kaleth was probably tired because of all my mistakes and got short-tempered. Takiza does it all the time to me. I'm sure it was nothing."

"Maybe so, maybe so," his friend answered.

But Barkley didn't say it as though he thought Gray was right. Not at all.

FLIPPERS
AND
FINS

CHAPTER 4

THE NEXT DAY, GRAY WAS SENT WITH BARKLEY and a cohort of twenty Aquasidor guardian finja to settle the territorial dispute on the edges of the Arktik Ocean between the orcas of Icingholme Shiver and Hideg Shiver, the sharkkind in the area. Apparently it was an age-old fight, and it was Gray's job to make sure it didn't erupt into a full-blown war.

Since they were in the open ocean, the greenie and coral grew far below them. The water was cold and deep blue for most of the way, and now there were giant floating masses of ice everywhere. The ice could be blinding white, deep blue or so clear you could see right through it perfectly. Sometimes it even magnified things, causing them to appear much nearer than they actually were. Gray couldn't fully enjoy the amazing wonders they swam past the way Barkley did.

Before they'd left, Takiza had told him, "This

41

assignment should be easy, even for you, so do not make chowder from it." Gray hoped he would do well but was unsure in this new leadership position, which relied less on battle skills and more on brainpower. Barkley would have been a better fit for this, but Kaleth wouldn't hear of that. She had let his friend come along, but told him to keep his mouth shut. The Seazarein's ongoing dismissive words and actions towards Barkley made Gray uneasy.

Why was she like that?

Barkley had put whatever feelings he had about Kaleth behind him. He was excited to be in the Arktik, an ocean he had studied but never visited. "Wow, it's cold here!" he remarked. "Look at that! More white ice! Does it get much colder?"

"Nah, once there's this much ice, it can't get too much colder," Gray answered. "At least not so we'll feel the difference."

"I like it," his friend answered. "Kind of refreshing."

The finja led them warily through the iceberg field, keeping an eye out for the attack they always thought was just a tail stroke away. They were led by the prehistore-size tiger-shark captain Shear, who never seemed to relax. Gray supposed it was a good trait for those protecting him. Most of the main types of sharkkind were represented in the finja: hammerheads, blues, tigers, great whites, bulls.

Most, but not all.

Gray had learned that the mako finja, led by Hokuu,

had betrayed the Seazarein on the day the passage between the Big Blue and the under-waters closed. Kaleth had almost died in that sneak attack, but Hokuu and the renegade makos had been beaten away. In the years after that, he'd tried to send her to the Sparkle Blue twice when she'd swum out to visit the ancient shivers. Since the last time, the Seazarein rarely left her fortified throne cavern within Fathomir.

"On the left, one thousand metres!" said one of the advance guard, a huge hammerhead. None of the guardians had been in their invisibility mode, but now they quickly altered their colouring. All these finja sharkkind, in addition to being massive, had other abilities. The power to shift their colouring like some starfish and anemones in the Big Blue was one of them. They were hard to see unless you were looking straight at them when they moved. And if they stopped, the guardians were almost invisible.

"Oh, I *wish* I could do that," Barkley said in wonder.

"Stay sharp," Gray told his friend. His own lateral line buzzed, mostly from the tension he felt coming off Shear and the others. It took Gray anxious seconds to spot why the scout had raised the alarm. "To the left by that big ice block," he told Barkley.

"I've got them," the dogfish answered. "Five, and ten more behind those."

Gray didn't say anything, but Barkley's sharp eyes had seen the other ten sharks before he did. Missing

43

this increased his nervousness about the mission. The fifteen fins swam towards them, unconcerned. A few did flinch when the guardians appeared from nowhere.

These were a mixed group of sharkkind. Pretty tough, but not tougher than the finja, and they knew it. The blue shark leader acted as if he wasn't surprised at all. Instead, he smiled broadly.

"Hallo there!" he said. "You must be Aquasidor Graynoldus. I've heard that your friends call you Gray and I'd like to be your friend, so hallo, Gray! My name is Palink, and I'm the leader of Hideg Shiver, also first negotiator in the dispute with Icingholme."

"Uh-oh," whispered Barkley under his breath.

Uh-oh, indeed.

Gray had a good idea as to why Palink had intercepted them before the meeting but would give the blue the benefit of the doubt. "We're heading towards the meeting area," Gray said. "Shouldn't you already be there?"

Palink laughed. "We like to be fashionably late. Besides, hovering with those flippers isn't our idea of a good time. They're such grumps, don't you think? Come on, we'll show you the way."

Shear cleared his throat. "We will set the path through these waters to the meeting area. It's *protocol*."

The blue shark dipped his snout in amused agreement. "Well, if it's protocol, by all means lead the way, my good fin." He turned to Gray. "So, was your journey pleasant? Smooth currents, I hope?"

"It was good. No problems," Gray answered.

"I'm glad we bumped into you like this," Palink told him as he swam closer so he could speak with Gray. They were almost touching flanks.

"Yeah, *totally* by chance," said Barkley.

Palink ignored that completely and kept smiling at Gray. It looked like the grin would split the blue's face down to his tail. "We've all heard the story of your heroic actions against that crazed flipper Finnivus and wanted to thank you personally. In fact, all the sharkkind leaders of the Arktik want you to know they're behind you one hundred per cent." Palink gave him a friendly tap to the belly.

Gray adjusted his position so he was a little further away from the blue shark. "Well, it wasn't as if we had a choice. Finnivus was coming to wipe us out. We had to win."

Palink swam in close again. "Interesting selection of words, that you didn't have a choice. Kind of like the situation we have here. If I may summarize the series of events, none of which were our fault, that have brought you here –"

Barkley cleared his throat, but Gray understood even without the warning. To negotiate with only one party in the present dispute would guarantee he would fail. "Palink, let's go to the meeting area separately," Gray told him. "If that isn't protocol, it should be. I don't want Tik-Tun feeling that we've been talking behind his tail."

Palink's smile remained, but his eyes changed, becoming hard. "By all means, Aquasidor Graynoldus. I only thought that since you're already such *pals* with Tik-Tun, we could get to know each other, at least a little bit, so he wouldn't have such a huge advantage. Because as it is now, I don't know if you've already decided things in his favour because he's your battle brother."

Palink turned sharply and bumped him as he led his group away. Though the blue shark leader would swear up and down it was an accident, Gray knew it wasn't. This wasn't a good start.

Gray and his fins got to the meeting place a few minutes later, and both Palink and his fins and Tik-Tun and his orcas were there. The water was cold and crystal clear. The two groups eyed each other mistrustfully from about ten tail strokes apart in a disputed stretch of water about half an hour from the Arktik ice pack itself. Immense blocks of white ice floated over their heads and blocked out the sun every few minutes.

Gray wanted to go and bump flanks with Tik-Tun, but as Aquasidor, that wouldn't have been the right move. *Especially considering what I've seen from Palink so far,* he thought. Instead, Gray began with the words that Judijoan had taught him for the occasion. "I am Graynoldus, Aquasidor of the Seazarein Emprex, Kaleth and I greet you both. I understand there is a dispute between you, and I am here to listen and offer advice. Speak now and be heard."

"It is good to see you, Gray," rumbled Tik-Tun. "It is a shame you had to swim so far on this fool's errand."

"If it's a fool's errand, there's only one fool here and that's you!" yelled Palink. "You're also a liar! There is no rival orca pod around here!"

The Hideg Shiver leader and Tik-Tun gnashed their teeth at each other. Their guards became tense, twitching fins and slashing their tails through the icy water.

Tik-Tun growled, low and deep in his throat, as he ground his teeth, which sounded like coral breaking apart. "Just because you didn't see members of our rivals, Glacier Shiver, swim through the waters doesn't mean they didn't! And call me a liar again, *fin*, and it'll be the last time."

Tik-Tun said "fin" like a swear word. It was odd and Gray had never heard that. To him being a fin meant you were cool or a good shark. But Tik-Tun didn't mean it like that at all.

Gray swam between the two. "That's enough!" He shook his head at Palink. "You really think that's the best way to begin?"

"Oh, sure, take your friend's side!" the blue shark sputtered.

Gray swung his head towards the orca leader. "And Tik-Tun, I expect better from you. If there's a problem with Glacier Shiver, you should tell Palink!"

"Flippers always stick together," Palink accused.

47

"This whole thing might be a plan to attack Hideg Shiver."

"Do you see? Do you see his mistrust?" the great orca said to Gray. "You ask me to treat with him in an orca matter? When he doesn't believe a word I say?"

"That isn't helpful, Palink," Gray told the big blue shark. "If it hadn't been for Tik-Tun and his battle pod, we would have lost to Finnivus."

"Yes, yes." Palink waved his tail dismissively, causing the giant orca to grind his teeth once more. "We've all heard the story of how brave Tik-Tun and the mighty orcas of Icingholme Shiver finally got involved in the affairs of the Big Blue. I'd like to know why. Why now, Tik-Tun? What advantage are you flippers looking for?"

"Are you going to let him insult me like that?" Tik-Tun asked.

"Look, he only wants to hear how you made the decision to help us," Gray began. He couldn't just avoid Palink's question, no matter how stupid it was. That would only make the Hideg Shiver leader more paranoid.

But Tik-Tun stiffened. "Perhaps I made a mistake in speaking up for you when you sharkkind needed help. I see now that fins will always stick together. Unless you need us to fight for you." With that, Tik-Tun and his orcas turned to leave.

"Where are you going?" asked Gray.

"Yes, where indeed?" Palink added. "I'm here to negotiate and solve the problem. But if you prefer war –"

Gray slashed his tail through the water. "Palink! Let him speak."

"I do not owe him an explanation, but you, Gray, I will tell," Tik-Tun said. "Icingholme Shiver must go to our southern feeding grounds. If we do not go, another group of orcas, such as Glacier Shiver, can claim them. We will be gone for two weeks. I will return if you think it is worthwhile."

"Peace is always worthwhile, wouldn't you say?"

Tik-Tun nodded. Gray turned to Palink, who was glaring at the orca leader. "I asked, *wouldn't you say*?"

"Yes, yes, of course," Palink answered. "Give peace a chance. We'll be here. You flippers can count on it. We won't be the reason this negotiation failed!"

Tik-Tun and his orcas swam away.

"Okay, good start," yelled Gray, trying to rescue the situation. "Let's build on this in a couple of weeks!"

Palink swam over, getting too close again. Didn't sharks know about personal space in the Arktik? The big blue got close enough to slap Gray's flank. "Once again we see why you should always be a fin, never a flipper." And with that Palink left with his guards.

That old saying got Gray thinking. He had said "Always be a fin, never a flipper" a thousand times in his life. When he was growing up in Coral Shiver, all the pups said it. Even the grown-ups did, for that matter. But he'd never actually *thought* about what it meant. When he was with Coral, and then with Goblin Shiver after that, Gray didn't even *know* any flippers, which included dolphins, whales, orcas and a few others. It was easy to think sharks were better than everyone else when he didn't really know any flippers.

But now he did.

Gray owed Olph the AuzyAuzy battle dolph his life, or at least his dorsal fin, many times over. The same with Tik-Tun and Icingholme Shiver. And the whales he met were usually smart and could sing so sweetly it would make you cry. So why was being a *flipper* looked down upon? Gray puzzled about this and found he didn't know. But he did realize one thing. He probably wouldn't be saying "Always be a fin, never a flipper" ever again.

CHAPTER 5

MARI SWAM DOWN THE SHIMMERING LAVA TUBE towards Velenka's prison in the Riptide homewaters. It was gleaming because Mari had ordered lumos to take up position every fin length, one every half metre or so, on both sides of the passage. You could swim down to the cells much faster now since you could see where you were going. The effect was weird. If you accelerated, the lumos blurred into a multi-coloured stripe that flashed past you: green, light blue, pink, red, dark blue, green, orange and so on. The sight should have been pretty, but the lower Mari descended, the more stale the water tasted. She felt sad for anyone kept in the prison, but Velenka had earned her place there.

Previously there had been only a few glowing anemones placed at areas where the lava tube bent and turned. They helped the sharks going down to avoid scrapes and bruises from brushing against the sharp walls.

None of the anemones who were there when the intruder had breached the defences of the Riptide homewaters had seen anything. But three *had* mysteriously died that night.

Mari didn't believe it was a coincidence. That was too much of a fluke.

"Velenka," she whispered to herself, scraping her teeth back and forth. The sleek, blacker-than-black mako was involved. But how? And why? Mari didn't have a clue. Now that she had finished deploying the ghostfins and had checked with Striiker – currently the leader of Riptide Shiver since Gray had been made Aquasidor – she was determined to find out.

Mari had thought Striiker would be pleased to be made leader. He had been, for a minute. But when everyone began looking to him for answers, it made him grumpy. Be careful what you wish for, Mari thought as she swam round the last bend before entering the prison cavern.

"Halt!" cried one of the two shiver shark guards in the chamber. "Identify yourself!"

"Mari, first in the Line of Riptide Shiver," she replied, slowing herself so she glided into the cavern in a non-threatening way. She was pleased to see that the two ghostfins she had placed inside were waiting in a high position above the lava tube's exit, perfect for striking an intruder's dorsal fin or tail.

The guard came to attention hover and dipped his snout. "I knew it was you, Mari, but you said –"

"You did well," Mari told the shiver shark, a small

hammerhead. "Don't trust your eyes. They can be fooled. The voice is harder, so always make them answer you. If they don't –"

"We attack," the guard said, gesturing to the two members of the ghostfins.

Velenka sarcastically slapped her tail on the smooth wall of her cell as Mari came into view. Even though there were five times the number of lumos in the prison cavern than before, the mako was still hard to spot.

"Playing big tough mariner today, Mari?" she asked. "Such a fun game for a pup! Can I play, too? I have lots of free time."

The young hammerhead glared at Velenka, about to lose his temper.

"Take a break," Mari told him. "I need to talk with the prisoner." The guard gave her a stiff head bob and swam up the lava tube with his partner. "You too." She motioned at the pair of ghostfins.

"We don't need a break," said the more senior of the two. He was looking out for her, Mari knew.

She gave them a more vigorous tail waggle this time. "Stay in the tube if you like, but give us some privacy."

The two ghostfins didn't like it but swam a quick half circle from their position and left the cavern.

"Seems like a lot of trouble to speak with little ol' me," Velenka mused.

Mari gave her a level gaze. "Much less trouble than

sending four of our mariners to the Sparkle Blue last night to speak to you, though."

Velenka hesitated for a split second before asking, "What are you rambling about?"

The mako kept her face neutral as Mari pressed, "It must have been hard for you, being at the mercy of that crazy fish Finnivus."

Velenka rolled her big, black eyes. "Please. You didn't listen when I told *you* that, and now you believe me?"

"It must have been tough, knowing that a misplaced word or chuckle could get your head on the emperor's seasoning platter."

"And?" Velenka asked. She seemed bored.

"And I'd hate for you to make that mistake again."

Velenka's needle teeth glittered in the colourful murk created by the anemones and lumos on the cavern walls. "What is it that you *think* you know?"

Mari paused to gather her thoughts. This wasn't going well. She knew from her time in Goblin Shiver that Velenka was one of the few fish in the sea who could make her feel stupid. There was no way she would win a battle of devious wits with the mako. Mari would have to tell the truth and hope for the best.

"I have no proof of anything, but something is going on. And I think it involves you."

Velenka nodded, not expecting this straightforward approach. It wasn't something she herself would have done. "Well, you're wrong," she answered.

Mari continued, "Gray didn't execute you even though you joined with one of the most evil fins the Big Blue has ever seen."

"When you say things like that, it shows how little you know about history," the mako said. "What about Kaangeson? How about Larvip the Life Ender? Or Oort the Unmentionable in Silander's court? Why, on any given day he –"

"Yes, yes!" Mari yelled, drowning out Velenka before she could tell the entire disgusting story. "We had four guards sent to the Sparkle Blue last night for no apparent reason. Tell me why, Velenka. Help me see that you've learned your lesson about telling good from bad." Mari swam closer to the whalebone bars and stared at the mako. "Are allies of Finnivus trying to free you to help in another bloody war? Do you really want a dark current like that flowing through the Big Blue again?"

"Finnivus is dead," Velenka replied. "No one is rushing forward to avenge him. You're flinching at shadows, Mari. Now, if we're done, it's time for my beauty nap." The mako turned away and wouldn't say anything else.

Mari left the prison cavern and went up the lava tube. The stifling feeling of the prison cavern seemed to coat her skin even when she reached the brightness of the Riptide homewaters. Something was going on, and she had no idea what. She would have to tell Striiker about her suspicions, even if they were thinner than the thinnest urchin spine.

CHAPTER 6

TAKIZA HAD MET GRAY, BARKLEY AND THE Aquasidor guardians as they were returning to Fathomir from the Arktik. When he saw the betta, Gray thought he was going to be yelled at for not solving the dispute. But when Takiza heard that the negotiation would continue, he wasn't mad. "That is time when they will not be fighting," he said. "Perhaps a solution will present itself."

It turned out that Kaleth had another mission for Gray and Takiza would be coming along. The betta thought it best that Barkley return to Fathomir with a few of the finja while he and Gray swam to the South Sific to manage a new dispute, this one between AuzyAuzy and Hammer Shivers. Gray knew the leaders, Kendra and Grinder, having fought alongside them in the war against Finnivus. How could they be fighting each other already?

Is this my life now? Gray wondered. Swimming

from one end of the Big Blue to the other, trying to calm disputes before they become bloody? It was an important job, for sure. But soon after they arrived, Gray wished *he* wasn't the one doing it.

Gray's head began to throb as the negotiation groups on both sides – with him in the middle – swam to the disputed area. It was always the same points, over and over. He wished his old friend Lochlan, the king of AuzyAuzy who had died fighting Finnivus's forces, was here, but that was impossible. AuzyAuzy's homewaters had still not fully recovered from the Indi armada's horrible attack, but there were signs of progress. New greenie bloomed, and the AuzyAuzy dwellers were repairing the torn and broken coral.

AuzyAuzy and Hammer's argument centred on feeding grounds, of course. Almost everything did when you got to the heart of the matter. Even if it were a personal dispute in which one leader was insulted or assaulted, the payment demanded was more hunting territory. Gray wondered what would happen if one day there weren't enough fish. What then? It didn't help that the landsharks were doing their best to sweep the ocean clean of fish and shellheads. What if the humans really got the knack of hunting in the deeper waters? Gray shivered at the thought and hoped he would never find out.

In this case the disagreement centred on a long-forgotten stretch of ocean that lay unclaimed between AuzyAuzy and Hammer Shivers near what they called the fire waters. The reason this territory went unclaimed was because in the time of Lochlan's father's father, there had been a huge volcanic eruption. For decades the area had seethed with choking sulphur which spelled death for any sharkkind who swam in it for more than a few minutes. So gradually, over the years, both shivers had stopped sending patrols and scouts there. The price was too high, and there were no rewards.

But sometime in the last ten years, the toxic brew boiling from the cracks in the seabed had stopped spouting in this area. A Hammer scout, wounded in battle and far off course, had drifted into the area and what she saw amazed her. It was incredible!

The silt and volcanic sludge that had blown up from deep under the ocean floor was ultra-fertile. It caused everything to grow at a furious rate. The greenie fields were towering! The coral fields giant! And it was beautiful! The colours were amazing: vivid blues, yellows, oranges, greens and reds. Coral lattices grew so fast they sometimes drifted away with the gentle current. And where there were coral and kelp, there were small fish and shellheads. And where there were small fish and shellheads, bigger fish came to hunt. Now this forgotten area had one of the richest food supplies in the entire southern Sific.

And both Kendra and Grinder wanted it.

Already their patrols had skirmished twice, resulting in three shiver sharks dying. Gray couldn't believe the friendship between the two shivers had deteriorated so quickly. Just weeks ago AuzyAuzy and Hammer Shivers had been allies against Indi's Black Wave armada. Now here they were on the brink of war because of something they hadn't even known existed a year ago! It was terrible.

Gray took in the striking expanse of vivid colour that both Kendra and Grinder wanted for their shivers. It was beautiful. He would have loved to glide past the delicate coral reefs, so newly formed, and bask in the warm, gentle currents. Of course, none of that was possible because no one was allowed to swim there due to the thick heads of the parties involved. And it didn't look like anyone was going to be able to.

Ever.

Takiza could usually be counted on to chime in with advice, or at least an insult, but had remained silent the entire time. He was content to let Gray twist in the current as both parties argued.

"I've already told you," said Grinder, the battle-scarred hammerhead leader of Hammer Shiver. "We won't give up the red greenie field without getting at least two of the coral reefs!"

"Those reefs are gigantic, and they're closer to our territory than yours!" replied Kendra, her voice rising. Gray had been sure that Kendra would be a great regent and leader for AuzyAuzy, but he had never seen this side of her. The whitetip had become so rigid in her views.

Maybe it would serve her as a leader, but he liked the old Kendra a lot better.

"If you want one of those reefs, then give us the valley –"

Grinder cut Kendra off with a slashing tail stroke, shaking his massive hammer head from side to side. "Why don't you just ask me to pull out my lower jaw and give that to you? Because you have a better chance of getting my lower jaw in this deal than *our* valley!"

"It's not your valley," Kendra replied in clipped tones. "We have ancient urchin maps and the valley is clearly included in our territory."

"Ya know where you can stick those urchin maps?"

"Stop!" Gray told them. "It's plain you two are never going to agree on how to divide this new territory. And it *is* new territory because no one has claimed it for so long."

"Doesn't mean a thing," said Grinder.

"I agree, with reservations," said Kendra. "I believe that the Seazarein, and you as her representative, will make a wise decision so that what you say *may* mean something." Jaunt, an AuzyAuzy mariner and Gray's good friend from the battle against Finnivus, seemed embarrassed at Kendra's words, switching her tail back and forth as she looked the other way.

What happened to you, Kendra? Gray thought.

"The Seazarein will make a wise decision," he told

them. "And since I represent her, I will tell you what it is soon. Very, very . . . soon."

"Any idea when?" asked Grinder.

"Are you hard of hearing? Soon!" said Jaunt, coming to Gray's defence. Kendra quieted the small tiger.

"Right. Soon," Gray answered. "Let's all hover in silence for a moment. She can sometimes speak to me by a, um, mind . . . link. But everyone has to be quiet."

Gray saw Takiza roll his eyes. The betta knew he had absolutely no answer. How could you divide something that neither party wanted to divide? It seemed the only way Gray could solve this dispute was to give the territory to *both* Grinder and Kendra . . .

That was it!

"Okay, the mind link worked. I have a solution, and if you disobey it, the might of the Seazarein's finja guardians and allies will make you wish you hadn't."

"You're threatening me?" Grinder sputtered. "We fought flank to flank!"

"Of course not," Gray replied. "What I'm telling you is that whichever side the Seazarein wants to win will win. Simple as that."

"So join me!" the hammerhead leader shouted. "I fought with you! Bled with you."

"So did I!" Kendra said, as she glanced at Grinder. "And if I remember, you came into the fight *after* we did! So if Gray's taking anyone's side, it would be AuzyAuzy's, where he swam diamondhead with our mariners in the victorious battle against Finnivus! Isn't that right, Gray? You haven't forgotten that, have you?"

"I will never forget either of those sacrifices! But what I think now is that the Seazarein claims this territory as her own!" Gray yelled. This got their attention.

"WHAAAAT?" cried both Kendra and Grinder as one, the first time they had done anything together in months.

"AND! AND!" Gray shouted over both sharks, quieting them. "Since the disputed area is what the Seazarein likes to call a *protectorate* of her merciful and wise leadership, she'll need someone to *protect* this new territory."

"And who might that be?" asked Grinder, giving him a hard stare.

"You –" Gray began.

"That's what I'm talkin' about!" shouted Grinder, switching his tail back and forth victoriously.

Kendra was quiet, waiting. She *would* be a good leader, Gray saw. "Let me finish, Grinder. It will be you and Hammer Shiver for one month, then Kendra and AuzyAuzy the next. This simple pattern continues until Tyro swims up and tells you that it's different. Understood?"

Grinder grumbled, thinking it over. "So, the Seazarein keeps her snout outta our business as long as we play nice. Well, I'm not happy."

"Neither am I," agreed Kendra. "In fact, I'm as unhappy, if not more so, than Grinder."

"And that's how you know it's a fair deal," Gray said. "*Both* of you hate it. So what should I tell Kaleth? Do we have a deal? Or do we have a war?"

"Fine," Grinder answered. "Been enough blood in the water this year to last a lifetime."

"I agree with the deal. *And* Grinder," said Kendra. "There's been too much war. Well done, Gray. Well done."

Jaunt nodded. "It's square an' fair, all right."

"I propose a victory hunt for you," Gray told them. "And after the new moon, neither side should ever meet in the Seazarein's protectorate. *Ever*."

"Yeah, yeah, we gotcha," Grinder said. "Don't make ya come back. We're not stupid, ya know."

"We just do a very good imitation of stupid," Kendra added.

Grinder roared. "*Very good imitation of stupid!* That's rich!"

"All right!" added Jaunt. "Let's cut the chibber-chabber and catch some fish!" And the sharks went off, friends and allies once more. When they were gone, Gray exhaled, long and slow.

Crisis averted.

Takiza nodded. "It seems you are not completely hopeless."

The betta was smiling when he said it, and that made Gray feel good. Maybe, just maybe, he wasn't the worst Aquasidor the Big Blue had ever seen.

BREAKOUT

CHAPTER 7

VELENKA WAS STARTLED FROM HER DOZE BY THE shouts of mariners far above in the Riptide homewaters. "Can you be quiet? I'm trying to sleep!" she yelled into the thin portal that gave her a small, circular view of the Big Blue. She did it out of frustration, really. The distance up the narrow opening was so great that there was no way anyone would hear. But if they were going to keep her locked up in a cell, the least they could let her do was nap, she thought. Velenka looked at the guards, who were suddenly alert. "Tell them to shut it," she ordered.

"I'll get right on to that," the larger one said sarcastically. He was about to continue when there was an explosion that sounded like a volcano had erupted underneath the Riptide homewaters. It shook the walls of the cavern. After the noise had died down to a rumble, the lead ghostfin told the others, "Move! Up the tube!"

Velenka slammed her tail against the whalebone bars of her cell to get their attention. "Let me out!"

But the guards were gone. Velenka tried to get a look at what was happening through the largest portal. It kept darkening and lightening, very fast. That meant many sharkkind were swimming past the hole. She strained to listen and faintly heard one voice over the others. "Get into formation! This is not a drill! Whatever went down there has to come out!"

Velenka knew that the voice belonged to Striiker, the great white who used to be in charge of training the Riptide armada. He was leader now that Gray was gone.

What was he talking about?

Went down *where*?

She turned to the cavern's entrance. Does Striiker mean down here? she wondered.

In answer the bodies of the ghostfins and guards thudded on to the rock floor. There weren't any bite marks, but all were surely swimming the Sparkle Blue.

Close behind their bodies, Hokuu entered the cavern. The frilled shark smiled a devious smile. "My dear Velenka, you look like you've seen a ghost. I told you I was coming. Did you forget?"

"H-H-Hokuu?" she stammered.

"That's an interesting way to say my name!" he answered. "Now let's get you out of here!"

Hokuu slid his tail through the bars and wrapped himself around three of the whale ribs. With an effortless pull, he ripped the ribs from their coral anchors. Velenka hovered where she was as Hokuu slid his tail over the side of her flank. She shivered at his touch. "You're free! Don't you have something to say to me?" he asked, waiting expectantly.

"Thank you?"

"Excellent," he hissed. "You have manners, unlike the sharkkind outside. But I will teach them manners." Hokuu gestured with his long snout to the cavern's exit. "Would you like to watch me punish them? Some revenge for keeping you in this dark, stinking place?"

Velenka's mind raced. What should she say? She didn't know. But she didn't want to be eaten either. In the end, the answer came easily enough. "I'd like that."

"Your wish is my very command," Hokuu said, his emerald eyes dancing like lanternfish. "But remember, since I'm doing this for you, you'll help me afterwards. That's fair, right?"

"Yes," she answered. Velenka had never felt as totally weak and powerless as she did now. Not even as a pup. "Of course."

"Then come," Hokuu ordered. "This will be fun!"

Quicker than she would have thought possible, the giant frilled shark disappeared upwards into the lava tube. After a moment, Velenka followed. Anything was better than being caged in a prison cell.

Or so she thought.

CHAPTER 8

"FINS UP AND AT THE READY!" BELLOWED Striiker to the other sharks from his position at diamondhead. All the training had really paid off. The two hundred Riptide mariners maintained their pyramid formation effortlessly. A reserve force of one drove was under the command of Quickeyes, and another hundred fighting sharks formed a perimeter behind the force led by Onyx. For a moment, Mari wished she was part of their armada.

But Mari was a ghostfin and she was proud of that. She didn't have the brute strength of most sharkkind mariners. But she was perfectly positioned in the greenie, hidden and ready to attack from the rear with Snork and the others, where they would do the most damage. The children and elderly shiver sharks, meanwhile, had been sent safely away under the leadership of Sandy, Gray's mother.

The prehistore snake-thing had swept past their defences easily, killing anything in its path. It seemed to move slowly, but that was only an illusion. The monster was lightning fast and deadly. Mari couldn't believe it! She recognized their attacker as an immense frilled shark. She thought that they only lived in the depths of the Dark Blue.

"On my mark!" yelled Striiker. The command was click-razzed by a battle dolph volunteer from AuzyAuzy Shiver. "Let's show this muck-sucker what's what!" There were whoops and hollers from the gathered mariners.

Then the monster appeared from the lava tunnel to the prison cells.

And he smiled!

"Is all this for me?" he said in a jaunty, unconcerned way.

"Give up and no one else gets hurt!" Striiker yelled. Mari couldn't believe that the big great white would even offer this. He had changed since becoming the leader of Riptide Shiver – he didn't want any of his mariners to swim the Sparkle Blue if it could be avoided.

The frilled shark laughed. "No, I don't think so! You see, I don't mind hurting you!" He moved his supple body, twisting it in an intricate pattern. A glowing globe of red light, crackling with energy, grew in the water where his body curled. Mari had seen Takiza do something similar when she and the rest of Rogue Shiver had fought Goblin and his sharks at the Tuna Run. But this energy was different from Takiza's. Its deep red shade was the colour of blood, and she could feel its malicious power growing as it gained intensity.

Striiker recognized the threat also. "Bull Shark Rush!" he shouted, and his two hundred mariners streaked at the monster.

The frilled shark flicked his tail and the ball of wicked energy blazed into the lower part of Riptide's formation. It seared through the ranks, setting any shark it touched on fire as if a volcano had coated it in lava! The heat caused the very ocean it passed through to boil. This scalding water roared upwards through the formation, killing every sharkkind it touched. In a moment more than eighty mariners were gone.

Somehow Striiker managed to avoid being sent to the Sparkle Blue. He shouted, "Re-form! Seahorse Circles Down!"

"See what fun this is?" yelled the nine-metre monster. For a moment Mari thought the comment was directed at Striiker and the rest of the Riptide mariners.

But then she saw Velenka! Mari had been right! The mako *had* been involved in the mysterious attack in the homewaters. She hovered by the entrance to the passage leading to the prison, her large eyes even wider than normal. "Hokuu, let's get out of here!" she yelled.

Velenka seemed frightened, but Mari's rage at the mako grew. I knew she was evil, Mari thought. And this Hokuu had to be stopped. But the frilled shark was too far away for her small force of ghostfins to make a rush from where they were.

Snork was close by and read what was in Mari's eyes. "We have to do something!" the sawfish whispered. Mari nodded and signed in the secret ghostfin language, twitching her tail and sending orders to move closer without giving themselves away. It would take a minute, though.

Hokuu released another blast of energy, this one an orange, explosive force that blasted Striiker and the Riptide mariners away, clearing a path from the homewaters. Hokuu cackled. "This is such good exercise!"

Quickeyes and his drove of mariners zoomed in, hoping to catch Hokuu while he laughed at what he had done to Striiker and the main force.

It was a false hope.

Faster than any sea snake, the frilled shark turned and faced Quickeyes and his hundred sharkkind. With a tail flick Hokuu released a blinding bolt of electricity that split into several branches. Each of those sizzling zigzags screamed through the water and hit a shark, the bolts passing through it and then another and another until almost every mariner there was struck. Quickeyes spasmed and slammed his jaws shut, breaking his teeth and drawing his own blood. Other sharks broke their spines. The eyes of many boiled away. It was horrible! The scent of burning sharkkind filled the water and its stench caused Mari to gag.

Striiker and his fins were still being tossed in the incredibly rough currents that the frilled shark was somehow creating. They couldn't regroup. Onyx gathered his defensive perimeter force and attacked. Hokuu twisted his body again. Another bright globe of energy gathered to destroy Onyx and the sharks with him.

She had to do something!

Mari gave the signal. They still weren't in a very good position, but the time for hovering unseen was over. "Attack!" she yelled. The ghostfins hurtled from their hiding places and formed a tight wedge. If Hokuu turned, he would see only one shark. But for now Hokuu's attention was on Onyx as he drew on his powerful killing energy. Mari, Sledge and Peen slammed into the frilled shark from behind, Sledge taking a chunk out of his slender eel body. Snork swam underneath Hokuu and cut him with his long, serrated bill.

"WHAAAT?" screamed Hokuu. "No one touches me!"

The glowing energy, not fully ready, zipped off and exploded at the edge of Onyx's forces. The damage was terrible but it could have been worse. Even so, what was left of those sharks was swept away.

Then the monster turned and fought the ghostfins snout to snout. His snapping jaws closed on one of the newer recruits, biting the blue shark in half. Hokuu's tail slammed Sledge away. Snork managed to dodge an attack but was thumped against the rocks below.

In seconds everyone around Mari was swimming the Sparkle Blue or so injured they couldn't fight.

Mari dived to attack again but the monster wrapped its coils around her flank, stopping her flat. Hokuu squeezed, and she felt her heart strain to keep beating. He drew her close to his mouth, filled with vicious, tritipped teeth.

"And who are *you*, exactly?" Hokuu asked.

Mari couldn't answer. She felt her life slipping away from the crushing pressure of the monster's might.

"That's Mari," said a voice behind Hokuu.

He turned. It was Velenka who had spoken.

"Mari," the monster growled. "Such a pretty name for my lunch."

She was drawn towards Hokuu's mouth.

"NO!"

Hokuu turned and the pressure eased. It was Velenka again!

"What do you mean, no?" asked Hokuu. "I give the orders around here, remember?"

Velenka's tail flicked back and forth, nervously. "I'm sorry," she said, dipping her snout in a sign of respect. "What I meant was, Mari was nice to me. The only one. Let her live."

"I don't know. She did touch me. Or one of her friends did."

"You killed the one who did that," Velenka told the frilled shark, her voice gaining strength. "Show this one mercy. Use her to convey whatever message you want to give."

Hokuu clicked his teeth together, thinking. "I've left the message I wanted to leave today." He gestured at all the destruction with his tail. "But I suppose I want someone to see what I do next to tell Gray and the Seazarein about it."

Hokuu slammed Mari to the seabed and began twisting his body once more. "Watch now as I destroy Riptide Shiver – forever!"

The frilled shark's body glowed with a malevolent orange colour. He released the energy with a flick of his tail and Mari waited for another burst of killing bolts. But it didn't explode.

The energy expanded and settled over the centre of the Riptide homewaters. Then the sickening orange energy became blacker than night, sucking the life from everything around it. The mariners trying to regroup began to twist and struggle because they couldn't breathe. The greenie and glowing coral lost its colour and shine as the lumos on the reef winked out, their colourful glows ending, one by one.

Then Mari lost consciousness and everything went dark.

CHAPTER 9

GRAY CRUISED WITH THE CURRENT, AT EASE FOR the first time in a long while. They were only a half-day swim from Fathomir and the sun was shining brightly, though the clear waters were cooler than those they'd left in the southern Sific. Gray had actually *solved* a problem in his position as Aquasidor! And both sides, while not exactly overjoyed with his solution, *respected* the decision. Not too shabby. AuzyAuzy and Hammer Shiver will *not* be killing each other next week, thank me very much, Gray thought. That was what he'd tell Kaleth, but in a more dignified way. Maybe he would do a little tail waggle after stressing all was well on the southern reaches of the Sific.

"So why was Taanglvos incorrect in his assumption?" asked Takiza, maintaining his distance from Gray's snout effortlessly without moving a fin. The betta had been interrupting the relaxing swim all day with questions

77

from his studies. Gray sensed that Takiza was actually annoyed that he was feeling good. Well, if that was the case, it would be the betta who was disappointed today. Gray hadn't missed a single question. Judijoan's constant carping must have rammed a load of knowledge into his head without his even realizing it.

"Let's see, that is so hard," Gray said, feigning to struggle with the answer, which he totally knew. It would be his fifteenth correct reply in a row. "You may have me with this one, Shiro."

Takiza wasn't fooled at all. "If you know the answer, simply say it. You very much enjoy blurting out incredibly *incorrect* answers. By all means, prove to me that you can blurt an accurate one from time to time."

"Someone is in a bad mood because of my winning streak," Gray said in a singsong voice, doing a barrel roll as he slipped into a cooler current. "How many is it, by the way? I wasn't keeping count. Oh, I remember, fifteen! So, my fifteenth correct answer in a row to the question 'Why was Taanglvos wrong in his –'"

"ALARM!" shouted Shear. "Protect the Aquasidor!"

Three guards jammed themselves above and to both sides of Gray. "*Oof*, is this really necessary? Can you give me a little room?"

"No," came the curt answer from Shear. When it came to his safety, the leader of the Aquasidor guardians was definitely in charge.

Takiza gazed deeply into the waters, looking into the

distance. Gray did the same. They weren't that far from the chop-chop, and the sun was so strong that there were flashes of reflecting light everywhere, making it difficult to discern anything. Then he saw.

There was a single shark, a hammerhead. The shark looked like it was drifting in the water. Then Gray noticed his tail moving, but slowly.

"Do you know this sharkkind?" Takiza asked him.

"I'm not sure," Gray answered, willing his eyes to see further. Even though the hammerhead was swimming at a sea snail's pace, he swam smoothly. "Wait! I think he's one of Barkley's ghostfins."

Takiza nodded. "Yes, I believe I recognize him. Sludge, or something of that sort."

"Sledge! You're right, it's Sledge!" Gray agreed. He bumped his way through his guards. "Let me through!" Sledge was a Hammer Shiver shark who'd chosen to stay with Barkley and the ghostfins after Finnivus and the Black Wave had been defeated. He was also one of the mariners who had accompanied Gray to the Seazarein's homewaters a few short weeks ago for his first meeting with Kaleth. But he and everyone except Barkley had departed with Mari.

What's he doing here? Gray thought as he swam over.

The finja who went out to make sure that Sledge wasn't a part of an ambush changed their colour so they were visible again. Shear told Gray, "I don't like this. He's bruised and burned."

Burned?

Gray moved closer to the hammerhead, who was barely conscious. He had several bruises on his snout and flank and one of his fins was charred. The hide there had dropped off, leaving light grey skin underneath.

Gray was horrified. "Sledge, what happened?"

The hammerhead opened the eye facing them. He hadn't stopped swimming, but he was so slow Gray didn't have to do much to keep up. "Is that you, Gray? Is Barkley with you? You – you need to come. Hurry ..." Sledge tried to turn and swim towards the Riptide homewaters, but Gray wouldn't let him.

"You're about to die from exhaustion!" Gray told the shark. "You're coming with us to Fathomir. It's close, and Barkley's there. You can rest."

"No time," Sledge replied in a rasp. But the hammerhead couldn't resist the two prehistore finja who guided him towards Kaleth's territory. "Bring Takiza. He can fight. We need everyone ... who can fight." Sledge faded out.

"What's he talking about?" Gray asked Takiza, who zipped down from his position and swam right over Sledge's snout. The betta brushed his frilly fins over Sledge's nose, causing the hammerhead to sneeze.

"Speak now," Takiza commanded. "Who would you have me fight?"

"Flip – flipper named ... Hokuu."

Worry gnawed at Gray's insides. "Why, Sledge? What did he do?"

"Destroyed Riptide homewaters..."

"What do you mean? What part?" Gray yelled, fear rising. "What part?"

Sledge mustered his strength and looked straight at them. "All of it."

Somehow, towing Sledge and fuelled by desperation, they made the half-hour swim to Fathomir in fifteen minutes. It took considerable effort by the Seazarein's personal doctor and surgeonfish before the ghostfin had recovered enough to tell the full story.

"Some of us, further away from the main homewaters, got out. But anyone caught in that black thing...they're gone."

Kaleth and Takiza shared a look as they digested the story.

Gray was shaken to his very core. All he could think about was his family and friends swimming the Sparkle Blue. For a moment he couldn't speak. He could not ask the questions. Is my mum okay? My little brother and sister, Riprap and Ebbie? The thought of any of them coming to harm was so horrible that Gray was paralysed.

Barkley stuttered, "Who – who got out? How many?"

"Don't know," Sledge said, struggling with his injuries and emotions. "Striiker ordered me here to make sure you all knew. Peen, Mari and Snork made it. Couple of others I fought with. But most of the regular mariners . . . they're gone."

So Striiker had survived. That was something. He would search for survivors and protect them, Gray was sure. "What about the far side of the territory? Where Razor Shiver used to have their homewaters? Where my – my family . . ." Gray tailed off. He felt guilty asking about his mother and brother and sister when he should be worried about everyone as he used to be their leader.

Sledge nodded. "Sandy hid all the shiver sharks when the alarm went up, and of course she didn't leave Riprap and Ebbie behind while she was doing it. They're okay. That spell, power, whatever it was – didn't get all the way there, thank Tyro. But the main homewaters and most of the hunting grounds, nothing lives there any more. Last I heard Striiker was gonna move everyone."

"Move them where?" asked Barkley.

Sledge seemed hesitant even to look at the Seazarein but did so now. "I think he's hoping to come this way."

"Great idea!" Gray agreed. "There's plenty of food."

Shear cleared his throat. Kaleth motioned for the guardian leader to speak. "That would be unwise. So many sharkkind in our territory would make it easy for Hokuu to slip past our guard." The Seazarein nodded, listening.

"But some are mariners," Gray pleaded. "They could help guard you."

Shear shook his head. "Those sharkkind are no match for even one prehistore mako finja, much less Hokuu, as we have just heard."

"You can't say no!" said Barkley. "You can't!"

"I can and will. The risk is too great. Hokuu can use the disturbance of your wounded forces arriving to pierce our defences." Kaleth gave Barkley a dismissive flick of her fins as if the conversation was over and turned to Sledge. "None of this would matter if he and his friends were competent mariners. They didn't even bruise Hokuu."

Sledge became angry. "It wasn't like we weren't trying! He ripped through us like a bunch of jelly drifters!"

Barkley slashed his tail through the water, signalling Sledge to be quiet so he could go on the offensive. "Kaleth, you knew about Hokuu and the threat he represented. You knew and didn't tell us, isn't that right? Tell me I'm wrong."

"Shut your mouth, dogfish!" Kaleth yelled. "We have been searching for Hokuu even as Gray and Shear have been maintaining peace. The frill is fiendishly smart, so it is beyond difficult to strike at him." She went on in a quieter voice. "Unfortunately, we did not see this attack against Riptide coming, or we would have been there to meet it snout to snout!"

"And keeping that secret turned out so well!" said Barkley.

"You didn't need to know!" Kaleth roared. Her finja

lined up in front of Barkley, ready to tear him apart on her order.

Barkley was incensed, his tail vibrating in rage. "Didn't *need* to know? Our friends are swimming the Sparkle Blue! And by the way, Gray and I are smarter than you think and we're from these waters. We might notice things that you could overlook. A wise leader uses everyone's talents to the fullest instead of bossing them around!"

"You're questioning my leadership!" the Seazarein thundered. "A dogfish?"

"Kaleth! Stop that!" Gray objected. "Barkley's my friend and I don't appreciate you acting this way!"

Barkley swam in front of him. "It's okay, Gray. Yes, Kaleth, I'm a dogfish. Because of that I see things in a different way. A way you've obviously never even thought of in your prejudice. And it's easy to spot a bad leader, like you. They don't listen to anyone because they're too busy yelling."

Kaleth vibrated with anger, but she wasn't about to prove Barkley right by shouting.

"I'll leave for Riptide right away," Gray told Kaleth, taking a more apologetic tone, "as your representative, of course."

Barkley nodded. "I'll go, too. Not like you want me around here."

Kaleth wasn't persuaded at all. "Neither of you is leaving! You'll stay here because it's my will!"

"That's ridiculous!" Gray answered. "Am I a prisoner now?"

"You are not a prisoner," Takiza told him. "But you are bound by your obligations. You must keep the shivers from fighting because if they do go to war, it will be impossible to enlist them as allies."

Gray ground his teeth until he heard one crack but continued listening.

The Seazarein didn't approve of Takiza explaining things, but she allowed it. "Mistrust and war favour Hokuu and his allies. If we require other shivers or Tik-Tun's orcas, and we well might, they will not join us if they themselves are at war. You cannot shirk your responsibility."

Gray spoke as evenly as he could, but he wanted to scream. "Okay. If I do that, then you need to figure out a way to stop Hokuu from doing anything else to Riptide."

Takiza drifted by the Seazarein. "Agreed. Hokuu would not have revealed himself in this way if it did not serve a purpose. The question we should ask ourselves is why he risked doing so."

The Seazarein calmed down, but her tail still pattered right and left in short, heated strokes. "Obviously he exposed himself to free this Velenka, who *should* have been sent to the Sparkle Blue." Kaleth looked straight at Gray. "But you showed *mercy*. Just what does this mako know about me?"

Gray was shocked. "Nothing! I wouldn't tell Velenka if the sun was shining!"

This seemed to soothe the Seazarein. Takiza swished his gauzy fins thoughtfully. "Gray knows well that she is dangerous. But it was common knowledge that we were coming to see you, even though we took a winding current."

Barkley shook his head. "Something about this isn't right. Velenka's smart, but Hokuu doesn't need her. No way. There's something else going on."

This time Kaleth didn't get mad. She ignored Barkley completely and spoke to Takiza. "That could only have been common knowledge if you had chosen to share the reason for the journey with these two." She gestured at Barkley and Gray. "Are you becoming a fool in your old age, Takiza?"

The betta gave no sign that he was insulted. Instead, he merely replied, "Apparently so."

"Then Tyro save us all," Kaleth muttered.

CHAPTER 10

VELENKA WATCHED AS SWIRLING MIST CIRCLED Hokuu and two massive prehistore makos she assumed were finja. She couldn't hear anything the frilled shark was saying. The glowing whorls blocked all sound from her ears inside the globe of energy. Apparently she wasn't a trusted member of his force just yet. This didn't stop Velenka from trying to read what was coming from Hokuu's toothy mouth. But in this she failed. She had been unfamiliar with frilled sharks before yesterday and couldn't decipher a thing he was saying.

After another moment the hazy globe dissolved into the blue waters as if it had never been there. She heard his last command. "Go now, and do not fail me." The two prehistore makos swam off. Hokuu came towards Velenka. His snake-like body wound through the water with a deadly grace that chilled her.

He can kill me whenever he wants, she thought,

fear coursing down her spine. After a moment another thought rose in her mind: so what else is new?

She had survived the unpredictable moods of the mad emperor Finnivus. And he'd sent people to the Sparkle Blue on the merest whim. Hokuu was better than that, wasn't he? Somehow she would find a way to not only survive but gain power.

But how?

"I trust your meeting went well," Velenka said.

Hokuu grinned at her, his emerald eyes glittering. "Funny word, *trust*," he said. "It's funny that you should say it, don't you think?"

His gaze unnerved Velenka. It was those eyes. They sparkled green, but weren't pretty. They scared her. She found herself making a conscious effort not to stammer. "Well ... I'm not laughing."

Hokuu chuckled. Ripples of laughter flowed through the length of his muscular body. "Oh, that was so delicious I'd like another helping!"

Velenka laughed with the frilled shark, but to her own ears she sounded flustered. If Hokuu noticed, he didn't mention it. "My dear, dear Velenka, what I mean to say is that trust is a current that flows both ways."

Velenka racked her brain. What had she done in the short time that they had been together to raise his suspicions? Nothing. In situations like these it was better to plead ignorance. In this case it had the additional bonus of being true.

"I'm sorry, but I don't understand," she told Hokuu, widening her eyes as if she were shocked that this was even coming up. This reaction had worked well on Finnivus.

But Hokuu wasn't Finnivus. Impossibly quick, he wrapped her in his coils and squeezed. "Please tell me that you're not stupid. Are you sure you don't understand?" All the while the frilled shark's smile never left his face.

Velenka found it hard to answer. She was being crushed. "You mean ... I have to earn your trust."

The coils unravelled and she could breathe again. Hokuu stroked her flank with his tail. His hide was silky smooth and felt slippery on her back. A tremor of revulsion went through her body. She disguised this with a coughing fit.

"You see?" he said. "That wasn't so hard. Don't play me for a fool and we'll get along famously. After all, I want you to be a valued member of my team!"

"To do what?" she asked timidly.

"Why, to establish a new watery world order, of course!" Hokuu said, flicking his tail with a flourish.

"I'm sorry," she said. "I don't want to make you mad, but really, I don't understand."

"Of course you don't! No one does except me!"

Velenka remained silent. She didn't want to take the chance of angering the frilled shark again.

He went on, "In ages past, the Big Blue was ruled by prehistores directly descended from Tyro and the

89

First Shiver. Of course my great species of frilled sharks was very important during this. Interestingly, we never evolved from our prehistore form, unlike everyone else. We're perfect, so why change, hmm? Anyway, when we great sharks ruled, there were no petty disputes and wars like the one that dear, demented emperor of yours fought."

"But what does that have to do with anything?" Velenka asked, genuinely baffled.

"It proves that today's Big Blue is a mere shadow of the greatness of what once was! But luckily, what was once *can be again*!" Hokuu smiled and waited for Velenka to comment, but she had no idea what he wanted to hear. "I can bring Fifth Shiver here to take over! It would have been done already if the passage between the oceans hadn't closed. I have my suspicions about what happened there, by the way, but they aren't important to you. What's important is that when I open the new passageway, Fifth Shiver will dominate and then eliminate the ineffective shivers here and the watery world will run smoothly again!"

Eliminate everyone, Velenka thought. He can't be serious. He can't. "But how would you do that?"

Hokuu's tail slipped from her flanks and he waved the spiky end from side to side in front of her eyes. "That's not for you to know yet! And this brings us back to the issue of trust."

"It does?"

The razor-sharp point of Hokuu's tail hovered close to Velenka's eye. "You were awfully interested in my conversation. A little too interested. I think you were spying!"

Velenka gasped. "No, no, I was looking –"

Hokuu whapped her on the forehead with his tail. Hard. "I need to trust everyone who serves me. If I think that you're playing games, I'll eat you alive. Do you understand this simple fact? Nod if you do."

Velenka did so as motes of light danced before her eyes from the blow. Then Hokuu slapped her on the flank with a loud *crack*. "Excellent!" he said, smiling once more. "I knew I could count on you! Now, get ready for some real fun. We're going to change the world, most likely replacing every fin with someone better!"

Velenka nodded. "Good plan. And you'll rule them all, right? Like the Seazarein?"

"The Seazarein?" Hokuu shook his head. "That young fool should be swimming the Sparkle Blue already. She hides inside the fortress of Fathomir, where I can't get near her. Not when she has all those finja around. It was blind luck she escaped me, and she had no idea until I struck. None. I was even her Aquasidor for a few short weeks before I struck. That's how stupid she and Bollagan were. If only Drinnok had come up before the passageway closed, then there would be no problems at all."

"Drinnok?" Velenka asked, puzzled.

"He's royalty and *sharkkind*, of course," Hokuu

said, his voice dripping with sarcasm. "Fifth Shiver still follows the ancient ways, so I need a royal to give everyone their swimming orders. But after a while, well, anything's possible."

Velenka found herself interested in the plan within a plan. She was a mako, after all. "So Drinnok will rule, but you'll guide Drinnok's fins. Help him . . . for a while." Velenka thought she had been too forward, but the frilled shark nodded his long snout.

"Exactly," Hokuu told her. "Bollagan didn't understand that in order to swim into the future, you must break with the past. He wants to live in peace with the sharkkind here. But Drinnok is a sharkkind with vision, proved by the fact that he agrees with me. I'll advise after I free him from the prison of the under-waters. It will all happen very soon." He looked up towards the chop-chop. The moon shone into the calm water, half full. "Oh, I can't wait for the moon to fill out. A full moon is beautiful, and that's when our beautiful new world will begin. One where we sweep away everything that's already here."

The frilled shark swam away, humming as he did so, his body rising and falling effortlessly with the current.

A feeling of despair engulfed Velenka.

Hokuu was mad. Crazier than Finnivus, even.

And the frilled shark was stronger than an armada of sharks.

What could she do? Velenka had no idea.

CHAPTER 11

"BARKLEY!" GRAY WHISPERED AS LOUD AS HE dared. "Barkley!"

The dogfish was nowhere to be seen. Gray and Barkley had slipped away to talk privately in the gold-greenie kelp forest of Fathomir, but then a patrol of finja had come looking for them. Gray had managed to hide but had lost his friend. He was still numb from the news they'd received from Sledge yesterday. Gray felt guilty about not having been there in Riptide's time of need. He was their leader!

Was.

Gray moved carefully through the massive stalks of greenie, making sure not to disturb them as he passed. He used his senses to keep well away from any large electric shadows, which he could feel but not see. They were the finja looking for him. They would find him eventually and Gray could only claim to be lost for so long.

"Barkley!" he whisper-shouted, trying to locate his friend. Even though the work he was doing as Aquasidor was important, he missed Riptide. He had pushed those feelings away to do what needed to be done. Now the homewaters were gone, and there was nothing he could do about it. He couldn't even leave Fathomir to mourn those who were swimming the Sparkle Blue.

The Seazarein wasn't going to let him. That much was clear. He was being followed everywhere. Kaleth said her finja would stop him if he tried to leave, and Gray believed her. But he could *hide*. Though the guardians were the best mariners he had ever seen, even better than Finnivus's *squaline*, Gray's training had given him enough skill to make himself scarce when he wanted.

Take that, Shear! he thought.

Had Barkley left? He was good, but Gray found it hard to believe his friend could have outwitted the guardians and sprint headlong towards Riptide without being discovered.

It was then he heard a "*psst*". Gray looked around for the source of the noise, which sounded like a small steam vent, though he knew it wasn't.

"Down here," Barkley whispered, so low that only Gray would hear it.

"What are we going to do?" Gray asked quietly. "As you may have guessed, those finja are pretty good hunters."

Barkley moved his snout out from the kelp he was

hiding in. He had a few strands of greenie hanging off it. The dogfish shook his head and most of the seaweed drifted away. "Yeah, I know, it looks weird. I got the idea from Takiza. I'm *being* the greenie."

"I want to go with you," Gray told his friend.

"There's no way I can sneak you out," Barkley answered. "And no, that's not a fat joke."

"I wasn't even thinking that!" protested Gray.

His friend's greenie-covered tail dropped with embarrassment. "Oh, you usually swim straight there."

"Not today!"

"Okay, sorry," Barkley told Gray. "But the fact is you're just too big and fat to sneak out of here." Gray snorted as the dogfish grinned. "You see what I did there?" his friend teased.

They chuckled for the first time since they'd heard the horrible news.

"Gray, you may have to listen to Kaleth, but I don't. What are your orders for me?" Then Barkley dipped his snout in respect – and he wasn't making fun!

Gray's heart swelled. "Obviously, get to Riptide Shiver, wherever they are. Remember, Striiker leads –"

The dogfish nodded. "I know, I know. Be less grating if I disagree."

"I mean it, Bark," Gray said, giving the dogfish a tap to the flank. "If he's making a bad call, you have to *convince* him, not argue him to death. He's not stupid."

"Never said he was stupid," Barkley answered. "And

he's got much better at listening to advice from what I heard from the ghostfins. A real leader."

Gray nodded. "Bring them here."

Barkley fidgeted. "Kaleth was pretty clear ..."

Gray cut his friend off, keeping his voice low. "And in this case I don't care. Either she provides protection for them, or I'm gone. Even if they send me to the Sparkle Blue, I won't ... I won't be a part of leaving Riptide out there undefended. I can't make mistakes like I did before."

Gray had once left his best friends in the world in Rogue Shiver and joined Goblin Shiver instead. Goblin had spoken stirring words about the need to band together, to protect each other, but it had all been an act. He had only wanted power. Gray shook his head at the memory. Though things had worked out since then, he'd never fully forgiven himself.

"Do you think we're creating another Finnivus in Kaleth?" Barkley asked.

Gray had never considered this. "I don't know," he admitted. "I hope not. But does a good shark turn away those in need?"

Takiza's familiar voice joined the conversation as he drifted between them. "She does when the fate of the entire Big Blue is at stake."

"We just *saved* the darn thing from Finnivus!" Barkley said.

The betta looked at Barkley and the greenie attached

to him. "Not what I meant. And Finnivus only had power enough to be a great tyrant. Hokuu has the potential to bring a mega-armada of prehistores into this world and destroy everything."

"Prehistores," whispered Barkley, his eyes widening. "I was hoping Kaleth was stretching the truth to get Gray to stay."

"She did not. Imagine five or ten thousand mariners as large as Gray and some much larger," Takiza explained. Both Barkley and Gray went silent. "So you can see the Seazarein's concern."

"But how do we know she's on our side?" Barkley asked. "I mean, *Kaleth* is a prehistore."

Takiza shook his head. "She follows her good king, Bollagan, who was sent to the Sparkle Blue by Drinnok. Drinnok will stop at nothing to be freed from the smaller ocean underneath this one. Thankfully, a seaquake sealed the rift."

Barkley looked over at Gray. "That must have been how you got here!"

"I guess," Gray said. "I don't remember."

"I have told you too much already," Takiza added. "Do not mention any of this to Kaleth. Her mind should not be cluttered by the past." The betta flicked a fin at Barkley. "Go to your friends. I have stunned the guardians and you should be able to slip away." Takiza showed the way with his tail.

"You'll be okay without me?" Barkley asked Gray.

"I'll muddle through," he told his friend. "Go. Bring them here. We're not following her command on this. No way."

Takiza shook his head but didn't disagree. "If you must. But that is sure to put Kaleth in a terrible mood."

"Then we're even," Barkley said. "Because I'm in a terrible mood."

And with that the dogfish left them.

BARKLEY'S JOURNEY

CHAPTER 12

EVEN WITH THE MAREDSOO THAT TAKIZA HAD given him, Barkley's muscles ached from snout to tail. He doubted he would have made it at all without the healing and endurance-boosting properties of that special, deep sea greenie. The Seazarein's kingdom was in the northern Sific and Riptide was in the southern Atlantis. While he knew the geography of the swim, Barkley hadn't been prepared for the actual journey.

In a way, it was wondrous. He had seen sights he had never imagined: the marching of millions of shellheads on the ocean floor as they migrated, schools of sailfish leaping in and out of the Big Blue, whales singing to each other from miles and miles away. It was incredible.

Other parts weren't such fun: cutting through the landshark waterway between the Sific and Atlantis, for example. They called it the Panama Canal. It was filthy! It had taken him an entire day to get the taste of oil and garbage out of his mouth. What exactly did humans think they were doing with their giant metal ships, polluting the Big Blue like that? You never knew with landsharks.

And we probably never will, thought Barkley.

But finally, he reached the edge of the Riptide homewaters.

It was horrible.

There was a dark haze covering most of the main area, including the once-grand Speakers Rock. Even though he was hungry, his stomach lurched because the waters stank of dead, rotting fish. As Barkley swam closer, he found it harder and harder to breathe. He reached a point where to go any further would mean heading straight into the Sparkle Blue.

Hokuu had created some sort of dead zone where the water wasn't safe. Some fish, mostly silver and brown "dumb fish", had gone into it anyway and died. They floated in the murky water, their lifeless eyes milky white. The glowing coral spires, once so beautiful, stood a gloomy grey instead of their usual vibrant blue, yellow, violet, green, orange, pink or red.

The reefs, once teeming with all sorts of dweller life, had no movement. Barkley could see the blackened and rotting husks of the lumos and shellheads that had had no chance of getting out of the area in time. The terraced greenie was all black and crumbly. And the majestic kelp curtain that had covered the cliffs overlooking the homewaters for centuries had turned brittle and white.

It moved stiffly, flaking off with every back and forth. Soon it would be gone forever.

Tears welled up in Barkley's eyes at the destruction and loss of life.

"You okay, sir?"

Barkley's fins and tail jerked, he was so badly startled. It was Peen, one of his ghostfins.

"I'm fine," Barkley said, shaking his head while trying to squeeze the tears from his eyes. "Good to see you're as quiet as ever."

"I had a great teacher," the small but tough hammerhead replied. Peen was too sharp an observer not to have noticed that Barkley had been crying but was a good enough fin not to mention it. "Would you like to hear my version of the battle on the way to Striiker and the others?" Peen gestured with his tail at the dead homewaters.

Barkley nodded. "Yes. Let's move away from here. The flakes are getting in my eyes."

"Those get in everyone's eyes, sir."

They swam away from the wrecked homewaters, and Peen told Barkley about the grisly battle between Hokuu and Riptide's forces. The camp Striiker had set up was about an hour away, and it took all that time for the hammerhead to fully explain the horror of the day. Quickeyes, the former leader of Coral Shiver, was dead! Their mariners had suffered almost two double droves' worth of losses, four hundred sharkkind, swimming the

Sparkle Blue. That was half of their forces! Barkley was speechless by the time a patrol of Riptide mariners found them. Seeing who he was, they took him to Striiker.

The big great white gave Barkley a friendly but sorrowful bump to the flank when they met. "Glad you're back. Maybe you can help me figure out our next move. Hovering here in the open isn't going to cut it. Once the last of the wounded are cleared for long-distance swimming, we're leaving."

Mari and Snork joined them. She swam with difficulty. But worse, her tail drooped and she seemed haunted. "It's good to see you, Barkley."

"Mari, are you okay?" he asked the thresher.

She nodded as Striiker hovered by her protectively. "Of course she's okay! You should have seen her, face-to-face with that demon frilled shark. Mari got a little squeezed, but she's gonna be fine."

"Yeah, she'll get better," Snork said, keeping a brave face. "You watch. We all will." Then the sawfish burst into tears. Mari patted him on the flank with her long thresher tail.

"We're thankful to have survived," she said. "So many others didn't."

It was clear that Mari was hurting from more than her injuries. The terror of the attack had left invisible scars as well. Striiker seemed at a loss, and even Snork was quiet. The great white motioned with a fin for Barkley to say something.

"So, Velenka," Barkley sputtered, saying the first thing that entered his mind. "Why do you think Hokuu wanted to free Velenka?"

"I don't know," Mari answered, grinding her teeth. "But it has to be something important."

"There aren't many sharks that I don't want to swim with," Snork told everyone. "But that Velenka? Something's *wrong* with her."

What did Hokuu want with Velenka? Barkley wondered. It was baffling. Why would the prehistore nightmare Hokuu need the mako at all?

"BARKLEY!" shouted a surprisingly loud but high-pitched voice. "It's really you!" The group turned as Yappy the sea dragon zoomed into their midst. "Now that Barkley's here, I bet we'll gather up everyone and stop that rotten sea worm! Boy, Barkley, you should have seen Striiker leading the mariners! He wasn't afraid at all! He went straight for them!"

Striiker snorted at Yappy's unsinkable enthusiasm. "Yeah, that didn't work so well, Yappy. But we're talking about important things here –"

The sea dragon flitted between everyone. "I know! That's why I'm here! I think we should ask my cousins from the Dark Blue to help us! They'd be great in a fight! Oh, you should see them! They're as big as Gray, and that ugly worm would wriggle into the seabed if he saw them! Do you want me to call them?"

"That's a great idea!" Snork said, waving his bill around excitedly.

"Sure, Yappy," Barkley said. "Why not? We can use all the help we can get."

Striiker was too busy shaking his head to even mind that Barkley was making the decision which should have been his because he was leader of Riptide Shiver. But who really cared who made the decision about Yappy's imaginary giant sea dragon cousins who lived in the Dark Blue?

At least everyone was smiling.

Then Barkley saw Gray's mum, Sandy, swimming over. She wordlessly glided over with tears in her eyes. "I'm glad you're here, Barkley. Does Gray know?"

"Of course he knows! He was worried sick about everyone here. Especially about you and –" It was then that Riprap and Ebbie made their appearance, zooming from under their mother's belly and pattering Barkley with baby snout bumps. "There you are! Your big brother misses you very much! You know that, right?"

Riprap let out a "yawwp!" and Ebbie nodded shyly.

"It was terrible," Sandy said.

Barkley looked at each of them. "Gray wishes he could be here with you. He really does."

Striiker snapped his tail in the water, loud. "Wishes? Wishes? Why didn't he come back? I can't believe he left us in the first place! We coulda used him in the fight, that's for sure! But to not come back now? Are you kidding me?"

"Gray was threatened by Kaleth so he had to stay put!" Barkley shouted at the great white. "He would have fought every finja in the place, but Takiza told him not to!"

"I don't like it, but Gray must have a reason," Mari said.

Sandy asked Striiker, "Do you really think my son doesn't want to help?"

"Of course not." The great white sighed. "I'm sure he feels terrible. I'm mad because I don't know what the heck to do. And I'm supposed to be the leader here. How's that for leadership?"

"Very good," Sandy told him. "Sometimes admitting you don't have the answer is the best thing."

"That still doesn't give us a current to swim," Striiker said. "We need hunting grounds for over a thousand sharkkind, their families and the dwellers staying with us."

Snork swished his tail. "Could we team up with Gray?"

Barkley nodded. "Exactly what he was thinking, Snork. We go to Gray's new pal, Kaleth the Seazarein. Oh, you'll love her, Striiker. So nice. And as you might have heard, she thinks I'm especially great."

"I can imagine," Striiker said, rolling his eyes. "I'm not joking, Barkley. We can't go there if the Seazarein is against it."

"Well, Gray says otherwise," Barkley told everyone. "We can't stay in Fathomir, but she didn't say anything about hovering next to her homewaters. It's the safest place you could find. And probably the only one that can feed us all."

"Barkley, I don't know," Mari said. "Won't Kaleth be angry?"

"Some sharks are angry no matter what," Yappy offered.

Snork nodded, and Barkley had to dodge his serrated bill. "Boy, that's the truth!"

"I can't believe I'm saying this, but *Yappy's right*," Barkley agreed. "Besides, who are we going to listen to? The Seazarein or Gray?"

"I vote Gray!" yelled Yappy.

"I like it," Striiker added. "Plus, we have no other options." The Riptide leader shouted to his mariners, "Form everyone up! We're going for a little fin-stretching swim to the northern Sific!"

CHAPTER 13

THE SEAZAREIN WATCHED IMPASSIVELY AS GRAY fought two of her best finja guards. Though they were well trained, if they hadn't had the element of surprise, Gray would have been more than a match for them. And one of the two was Shear, the captain of her guardians. Gray put his superior size and quickness to good use, ramming the prehistore tiger in the flank before ploughing the other, a bull shark, into the seabed below. The two finja guardians dipped their snouts to her and left as Gray waited for her judgement.

Kaleth stretched her fins. "It seems you can take care of yourself in a fight. For that we can be thankful, at least."

"He also did passably well in solving the dispute between AuzyAuzy and Hammer Shivers," Takiza reminded her.

Kaleth tilted her head to Gray, acknowledging this.

111

"There are other matters in the seven seas that haven't been solved, such as the disagreement between the orcas and sharkkind in the Arktik. And Hokuu is an entirely different subject. I doubt he will show himself outside our borders and challenge either of you to single combat."

"Agreed," Takiza said. "We should not wait for that."

"If Bollagan were here, he would end this in a day," Kaleth declared, slapping her tail against a massive formation of green brain coral. "He would know what to do."

"Wait, so he's alive?" Gray asked, genuinely curious.

The Seazarein was puzzled, but Takiza was staring icy death at Gray.

Oh, he told me not to say anything about that! Gray realized too late. The two-against-one fight with the finja had taken a lot out of him, and he was dizzy from the effort. But Gray knew he had just made a big mistake.

"What do you mean?" Kaleth asked. "Why do you think Bollagan is gone?"

"He means nothing!" Takiza snapped. "He once again speaks when he should remain silent!"

Kaleth stared at Gray, her eyes boring into him. He tried to cover his mistake and stammered, "I don't know. It's – it's been a while since you've talked, right?"

The Seazarein swam forward. Kaleth was a good tail fin larger than Gray. He didn't know if he would win in a fight if she attacked him. She gazed levelly at him and asked once more, "Why do you think Bollagan is dead?"

"I – I don't know!" Gray said, but his eyes went to Takiza.

Kaleth put everything together and whirled to face the betta. "My king is dead! And you knew!"

The guardians appeared, but the Seazarein flashed her tail for them to go. "Leave us!" she shouted.

"By chance, I was in the under-waters as it happened," Takiza told her. "I could do nothing."

The Seazarein's mighty tail drooped. She allowed herself to sink almost to the ocean floor. "My king swims the Sparkle Blue."

Gray saw that Kaleth must have greatly respected, even loved, the leader of Fifth Shiver. She swished her tail morosely, causing sand to swirl upwards. She peered at the fine grains of silt as they floated around her. "So, Astol is the new leader of Fifth Shiver. He's a bit prissy for my taste, but intelligent, I suppose."

Takiza shook his head. "Astol does not lead. Drinnok does."

This got an immediate reaction from Kaleth. She shook her massive fins and swam in a slow circle, thinking furiously. "Impossible! That brute was fourth in the Line. He could never have beaten Bollagan or Graynoldus in single combat! And then there's Jokinin – he'd have to worry about her, too."

"Drinnok staged a coup, Kaleth," Takiza told her gently. "He killed Bollagan, and his frilled mariners sent the rest of the Fifth Shiver Line to the Sparkle Blue."

"All this time and not a word about this?" the Seazarein roared. "Why didn't you tell me?"

Takiza didn't reply and during the silence Gray asked, "Who's Graynoldus?"

Kaleth looked at the betta, then him. "And now this."

"I had hoped to avoid this and many other things, but the current flows as it will," Takiza replied.

The Seazarein explained, "Graynoldus was your father, Gray. He was royalty and served in the Line of Fifth Shiver. You look very much like him. He was a good shark."

"So this takeover happened and my dad got me out?" Gray asked. It didn't seem possible. "Is he . . . alive?"

Takiza shook his head. "He would not have sent you through the passage alone. If he lived, he would have joined us at Fathomir."

Kaleth scowled at the betta. "It was you," she accused. "It wasn't an earthquake that sealed the passage. It was *you.*"

"I had no choice," Takiza confirmed. But he didn't ruffle his fins as he did when he believed himself right. Plainly, the decision weighed on the betta. "There was chaos. Bollagan and his allies were dead. I heard Drinnok planned to invade the Big Blue that day. The fins following him all shared the opinion that these waters should be conquered by Fifth Shiver. I had to seal the passage."

"And you didn't trust me enough to say anything," Kaleth stated.

"We had known each other for only a short time," the betta told her. "I do apologize. But I could not take the chance that you might agree with Drinnok's point of view."

Kaleth frowned. "All this time you've been whispering in my ear, offering advice. All this time. And you said nothing!"

"You shouldn't be mad at him," Gray put forward.

"SILENCE!" roared the Seazarein. "You are my Aquasidor and have a dispute to solve for me in the Arktik!"

"I will attend him," Takiza said, dipping his snout.

"You will not!" Kaleth yelled. "It's high time we see if he can do this job alone. You'll stay and tell me everything you've been hiding."

Takiza gestured at Gray. "Do not punish the boy for my actions."

"You forget yourself!" Kaleth shouted. "Either come with me now or never swim into Fathomir again! Choose!"

"I can do it," Gray told the betta as confidently as he could. "Shiro, I can." He nodded far too many times, though. Any chance they had of stopping Hokuu would be ruined if Takiza and Kaleth weren't allies, so Gray couldn't allow that. Not when opening his big mouth was the reason for the fight.

The betta nodded and dipped his snout to Kaleth. "I am here to serve," he said.

"You'd better be, Takiza!" she answered, swishing her tail in short, angry strokes. "You'd better be!"

CHAPTER 14

VELENKA PEERED UPWARDS FROM HER HIDING place in the thick greenie as the Riptide Shiver sharkkind passed by. Though she hated sticking her snout in the sand like some muck-sucker, sometimes it was the best thing to do.

Especially today.

"Don't be such a turtle," hissed Hokuu, floating above her. A little higher and they would be spotted for sure because the water was frighteningly clear here. And the Riptide mariners – at least the ones called ghostfins – were good at hiding and launching surprise attacks from the abundant greenie in the area. That was a combination that Velenka didn't want to try her luck against.

Hokuu sensed what she was thinking and remained unconcerned. "You believe these pups can see through my powers? Think again, dear."

Indeed, there was a hazy film encircling them that

the frilled shark had created. Velenka began trusting it more when a scout passed no more than ten strokes off to the left. Even if the bull shark was half blind, he should have detected them.

Velenka relaxed. "You're right again, Hokuu."

The frilled shark sent a series of intricate ripples cascading through the length of his body. "Of course I am." He turned those unsettling emerald eyes on her once more. "Rely on that. I'm always right."

Velenka fidgeted, flexing her fins, but said nothing.

Hokuu whipped his tail against her side, causing her to start. "What is it?" he asked in a low voice. "Something is on your mind, and you'd be wise to tell me this instant."

"I don't know what I'm doing here!" she admitted.

The Riptide mariner heard Velenka and streaked towards them. Suddenly Hokuu was gone and the filmy haze in front of her disappeared. The bull shark saw Velenka and shouted "You! It's y–"

Hokuu's tail speared the shark through the gills and he bit the scout's head off before the bull could finish his sentence. The frilled shark waved his pointy tail at Velenka in a no-no motion.

"*Shhh*," Hokuu hissed as the transparent barrier again took its place around them. "Just because they can't see us doesn't mean they can't *hear* us. Different katas in shar-kata do different things, and this one is good for hiding in plain sight."

Velenka lowered her voice. "I apologize. But what's on my mind is still the same."

"You're helping me bring about a new order, Velenka."

She saw no way out of asking more questions of Hokuu. That could get her killed. But not knowing what she was supposed to be doing could also get her killed. Velenka sighed. "Yes, you've said that. But I still have no idea what role to play. You have unbelievable powers. Finnivus and his entire armada would be no match for you. How could you possibly need me?"

"Because I have to speak with Kaleth and I can't while she's hiding in Fathomir. That's what Bollagan named their homewaters here. Stupid name, but very defensible. It would be too risky for me to try a frontal attack. I have to even the odds a bit. And then there's Takiza – he's another problem." The frilled shark made a loop with his tail. "It's all connected. The Seazarein is connected to Takiza, who's connected to Gray, who is connected to *you*." Hokuu tapped her between the eyes with his razor-sharp tail. It still had the scent of the scout's blood. "You're friends with Gray, aren't you?"

Velenka ran through every possible answer. Her first impulse would be to lie and say yes, but she had a feeling this was a test. One that, if failed, would leave her swimming the Sparkle Blue.

"You know I'm not," she answered.

Hokuu smiled. "I *do* know that. But I also know that

you *were* friends. And I know he'd like to talk with you."

"I tried to manipulate Gray before," Velenka said, thinking back to their time as members of Goblin Shiver. "In every way possible. I separated him from his friends. I had him placed in Goblin's Line. Nothing worked! He figured out I was up to something." Velenka chuckled. "I hate to say this, but that big, dumb fin managed to outsmart me."

"You're going to figure out a way to talk to Gray when he gets here."

"So Gray will come this way? To us?"

Hokuu's eyes glittered. "Of course he will. Like I said, it's all connected. Gray loves Riptide. He cares about his friends too much."

"But what will I talk with him *about*?" she asked.

Hokuu's tail whipped underneath and smacked her smooth belly, causing Velenka to slam her mouth shut. "Stop talking. You don't want to convince me that you're useless, do you? Not when we're so close."

Velenka shook her head. "No, that's not what I want." She wasn't satisfied at all with the frill's non-answer, but there was nothing she could do about it. Velenka smiled and nodded, knowing that she was powerless.

"Good, because when the moon is full, it'll all be over. Just a week. Gray will come, you'll see. And then I can have my chat with Kaleth!" Hokuu said, his own voice rising. Two Riptide mariners swam over to investigate. "You figure out how you're going to help me . . . and I'll start making Riptide Shiver bleed to draw Gray here."

Hokuu turned and jetted at the mariners. He wrapped both of them in his coils and snapped their spines with a sickening *craaack* that vibrated through the waters. Alarms went up from the other scouts. "Let's have some fun!" Hokuu yelled.

Then there was screaming and blood in the water.

Velenka pressed her snout into the seabed and wished she was back in her whalebone prison cell.

CHAPTER 15

GRAY WAS GLAD THE JOURNEY TO THE ARKTIK was a long one. The icy blue water slowed the thoughts swirling in his mind, and for that he was thankful. Neither Shear nor any of his squad chose to speak to him, and that was okay since he wasn't in a talking mood.

Gray hadn't asked to be the Seazarein's Aquasidor. If Kaleth decided to give the job to someone else, she wouldn't have to ask him twice if he minded. All she would see was a bubble trail as he rocketed away to rejoin Riptide Shiver. But if Takiza and Kaleth thought he was the best one to keep the peace, he would try his hardest. If that helped them stop Hokuu, Gray would do everything he could as Aquasidor.

Gray chuckled sadly. When he had been growing up with Barkley in the warm, peaceful Caribbi Sea, he would whine constantly about the lack of action and adventure there. Coral Shiver's reef had been so peaceful and quiet! Days would pass with nothing at all happening but the sun shining into the water.

What a huge chowderhead I was to complain, Gray thought.

It wouldn't do to bellyache now, though. He was older, and things were expected of him. But a day or two spent lounging in the Caribbi would be great. He would even settle disputes if anyone asked. Gray could see himself now, solving a big argument between the shellheads and urchins over who got to eat a squid who had died of old age. That would be sweet ...

"There's a problem, Aquasidor," said Shear.

"Huh?" Gray's daydream had been so complete he almost bumped into Shear, who had stopped dead in the water. He recovered and hid this by harrumphing, "Yes, of course there's a problem. That's why the Seazarein sent me."

The prehistore tiger rolled his eyes and gestured with a fin. "No, we have a problem because it seems that a war is beginning right this minute."

Gray looked past Shear's flank and saw an armada of at least two hundred sharks facing off against two battle pods of orcas!

"For the love of Tyro!" Gray huffed. "I *told* them not to do that!"

"Seems they didn't listen," Shear answered.

Gray slashed his tail through the water. "We can talk about your sarcasm later, Shear. But right this second, how about we stop this stupidity from happening?"

Shear snapped to attention hover and dipped his snout. "Orders, sir!"

"Bull Shark Rush, straight in. Keep them from fighting, but don't hurt anyone." Gray considered how far he should go. He had to make it clear this sort of thing wouldn't be tolerated. "Shear, what I mean is keep yourselves safe and don't hurt anyone *permanently*."

The tiger guardian leader cracked a smile. "You heard the Aquasidor! Bump and bruise, nothing more!"

"Let's go!" shouted Gray. He switched his muscular tail back and forth, accelerating into an attack sprint. The frigid water whisked past his gills and Gray felt more focused than he had in weeks. He wouldn't let these two groups go to war. That would be good for Hokuu and bad for everyone else. "Not on my watch," Gray muttered as he angled towards Tik-Tun.

It took two hundred tail strokes to get within shouting distance. "Stop! Stop, I say!"

Tik-Tun saw Gray as he skidded to a halt in front of his hundred orca mariners, all ready for battle. "It's too late! We will defend ourselves!"

Gray circled so he had a better view. Palink was swimming the diamondhead, and Hideg Shiver's triangular formation was gaining speed.

"Give it a second," he told the orca leader.

Shear's twenty finja smashed right through the entire Hideg Shiver formation from one end to the other. The guardian captain was good as his word. Though the finja bumped, rammed and tail-whipped any mariner in their path, none were hurt. Well, none were *permanently* hurt, though more than a few drifted unconscious in the clear, cold water.

The entire formation collapsed. Palink was mashed between Shear and another finja and brought before Gray and Tik-Tun. The blue shark was furious. "Treachery!" he shouted. "How could you turn on your own kind? I knew you were a flipper at heart!"

Gray wanted to tail slap Palink so hard that he'd spin for a day. However good it might feel, that wouldn't help solve this problem. Instead, he gnashed and ground his teeth. In the quiet waters between the two forces, it sounded like rocks tumbling in a strong current.

"I judge everyone I meet the same way. Are they a chowderhead or not? And you, Palink, in addition to being prejudiced, are a chowderhead."

"What?" Palink sputtered. "You can't call me that! You're the Aquasidor – you can't favour one side over another! I'll report this to the Seazarein!"

"I speak for the Seazarein!" Gray roared. "I told you to wait and instead you gathered an armada!"

Palink's tail drooped and, to his credit, he looked somewhat ashamed. "Well, the flippers –" Gray gave Palink a steely stare and the blue shark corrected himself. "The orcas were going to take our best hunting territory for themselves!"

"Untrue," growled Tik-Tun. "We had just come back from our journey. Some of my pod did hunt, but only to eat during the swim."

And then it came to Gray. The solution he was looking for! He had been thinking too much like a shark and not enough like an orca. Or, he thought guiltily, too much like a *fin* and not at all like a *flipper*.

"I've discussed your problem with the wise and all-knowing Seazarein." Gray couldn't believe he'd just said that, but it wouldn't hurt for both groups to think that Kaleth was a good ruler. "If you'll swim with me, I'll tell you what she recommends."

Palink had a nice bruise darkening his snout. "By *recommends*, do you mean *orders*?" he huffed.

Gray smiled, grinding his teeth, but quietly this time. Palink could be such a tailbender! "Why don't you listen first?"

In the end, both sides were not only satisfied; they were actually happy! Gray divided the disputed territory into thirds, two-thirds of which went to Hideg Shiver. They had many more mouths to feed, after all. Since orcas were different from sharkkind in that they didn't actually *want* a set territory, that didn't matter much to Tik-Tun and his pod. But this way, they always had a place that Palink and Hideg Shiver would never set a fin inside.

Here's where Gray's stroke of, if not genius, at least good thinking, came in. Orcas migrated in search of better hunting, and it didn't always occur on a set schedule. What Tik-Tun and the orcas received was the right to travel across Hideg Shiver any time they wanted as long as they gave one day's notice. And when they were away, Hideg Shiver could hunt in the remaining third of the disputed territory, which they had to leave promptly when the orcas returned with the same one-day notice being given. It worked for everyone.

Palink gave Gray an embarrassed look when they reached the end of the negotiations. "I can't believe I was going to start a war when there was a bloodless solution this good."

"It is truly a wise decision," rumbled Tik-Tun in his deep voice. "I have come to expect nothing less."

"Oh, you expected less, Tik-Tun," answered Gray. "But I'm glad to beat your expectations this time."

"I'm sorry for causing this trouble, Gray," Palink said. "You're right about me. I *am* a chowderhead and unworthy to be Hideg Shiver's leader."

"A good leader is one who recognizes his mistakes," Gray told the blue shark. "And everyone can be a chowderhead from time to time. Ask my friend Barkley. He thinks I'm one on almost any given day."

The three laughed together. Palink bowed to the orca leader. "Tik-Tun, I haven't been a friend to the orcas, or any who swim with flippers through the Big Blue. But

I'm willing to try and change my ways. I humbly ask you for the chance."

"You shall have it, leader Palink," rumbled Tik-Tun. "I am also guilty of these types of thoughts regarding sharkkind. Once begun, they are hard to stop."

Gray gave each a tap to the flanks. "I think you two could change that. If you're willing to work together."

Gray smiled when Tik-Tun and Palink nodded in agreement.

Sometimes, being the Aquasidor wasn't half bad.

RIPTIDE REFUGEES

CHAPTER 16

THERE WAS BLOOD IN THE WATER. GRAY COULD smell it, as could everyone in his entourage. They were tired from the punishing pace they had settled into, but he was happy to be away from the floating ice of the Arktik. This should have been a nice, stress-free swim towards the Seazarein's territory, where some other huge problem was undoubtedly waiting. But trouble was already swimming just ahead of them.

When Gray first smelled the blood, it was faint and he ignored it. The Big Blue was the Big Blue, and fins and dwellers were either having lunch or being lunch. That was the way of the watery world. But then the guardian scouts, who travelled ahead of the group, came with news. It wasn't the blood of one shark or dweller. There were many different types. Too many kinds and too much of it.

Gray had to investigate. Even before he had been

KINGDOM OF THE DEEP

Kaleth's Aquasidor, he couldn't have ignored this. He ordered Shear to increase their pace. It was another day before Gray saw the mass of sharkkind. Their mariners had a solid defensive screen, but inside that were many older shiver sharks and pups. And though blood was thick in the water, there was no attacking force that Gray could see for a long while. But then there was a disturbance.

"Their rear guard is being attacked," said Shear. He, like the other guardians, was nearly invisible. Gray peered into the distance. He couldn't see anyone striking, but the mariners *were* fighting someone.

Gray realized who the mariners were at the same time Shear said, "Finja! The renegades!"

"It's Riptide and they're being attacked!" Gray told him. "Help them!"

"No, the danger is too great!" Shear answered, shaking his snout. "We must withdraw."

"Do what you want!" Gray said as he accelerated into an attack sprint, bursting through his barrier of guardians. "But I'm not leaving my friends!"

Shear had no choice but to follow. "Protect the Aquasidor at all cost!" he shouted as he caught up with Gray. The water was murky and provided some cover. Gray could see the dim outlines of Hokuu's mako finja assaulting the outclassed Riptide defenders.

Gray shouted, "*Riptiiiide!*" as his small force crashed into the fight. Using his senses as Takiza had taught him, he could feel the electric shadow signals of the

132

renegade makos. Each sharkkind had their own image, and because of this Gray could separate friend from foe. He rammed one attacker and Shear took its fin.

The makos were surprised. It looked like they would be scattered, but they were too skilled for that. Instead, ten more joined the fight. At least they were concentrating on Gray and his guardians and not the sharkkind of Riptide. Soon there was a chaotic battle with roaring charges and flashing teeth everywhere.

In all the confusion Gray was swept clear of the heaviest fighting after he bit the tail off a prehistore mako finja and sent it spiralling towards the seabed. It was tough to send them to the Sparkle Blue, but it could be done. As Gray turned to rejoin Shear and the rest of his guardians, a huge horror rose in front of him. The monster's flexible eel-like body was longer than his by a good three metres and had a spike on its tail.

Gray's eyes widened. It was Hokuu!

The frilled shark knew what he was thinking and replied, "Yes, it's me."

Hokuu struck with his tail, tapping Gray between the eyes. Gray was paralysed! He couldn't move a muscle!

"Let's talk," Hokuu told him with a horrible, toothy smile. A misty wall encircled them both. "I like a little privacy when I'm speaking with a friend."

The battle a few tail strokes away reached fever pitch, but no one could see them. Gray found he could move his mouth enough to speak. "I'm not your friend. You're evil!"

Hokuu looked positively wounded as he balanced Gray on his tail so he wouldn't drift to the sand below. "I'm not evil. Just misunderstood."

Gray struggled against the paralysing touch Hokuu had given him. He had seen Takiza do the same thing. It wasn't fun, but it was temporary. When it wore off, he would attack.

Keep him talking, Gray thought. "The Seazarein knows your secret plan. She won't allow you to let Drinnok and the other prehistores into the Big Blue to kill everyone."

Hokuu snorted. "Secret plan? Maybe secret from you. They don't tell you much, do they? Both Kaleth and Takiza love to keep secrets."

Gray forced his fins to flex. They did, but only a little. And he couldn't move his tail at all. "Takiza stopped you once. He'll do it again."

Hokuu laughed. "My former Nulo? Oh, please! That mincing dweller is no match for me! The only reason little Taki can even feed himself is because I taught him how."

Gray felt anger rising, hot in his throat. No one spoke about Takiza in that way but him! "You'll pay for the Riptide sharks you sent to the Sparkle Blue and everyone else you hurt! I swear it!"

"But they attacked me! I'm the injured party here," Hokuu said, gently bouncing Gray up and down with his tail. "And if you're going to avenge deaths, you'll need to fight Taki, also. Did you know he killed one of his apprentices just for talking back? Snapped his spine like that!" Hokuu made a cracking noise by flicking his tail in front of Gray's snout.

"You lie! Takiza would never do that!"

Would he?

Hokuu drew close and Gray could see the dangerous, tri-tipped teeth filling his mouth. "If you aren't going to stick up for a fellow apprentice, that's fine by me. But what about your father?"

"What do you even know about my father?" Gray spat. He still couldn't move his tail although he was twitching his fins furiously.

"Takiza killed him," Hokuu said, his green eyes sparkling in the cloudy red water. "You didn't know? Yes, Taki did stop the prehistores from coming through. But he *killed* your father doing it!"

Gray could only whisper, "No."

"Oh yes," Hokuu said, drawing even closer. "He knew you and your father were in the passage and still closed it! It was a miracle you survived at all! I'll bet he didn't mention that during any of your training sessions, hmm?"

Hokuu moved off and the misty barrier began to

dissolve. "Say hi to Taki for me when you speak with him. Until we meet again, Gray!"

And with that Hokuu disappeared along with the mako finja.

The fight was over, for now.

CHAPTER 17

THE DEEP BLUE WATER TURNED DARK AS NIGHT fell above the chop-chop. Of Hokuu and his renegades there was no sign. The Riptide sharks moved as quickly as they were able towards Fathomir, but then had to stop. The wounded could go no further, and many of the younger and older shiver sharks hadn't eaten in days. Striiker ordered heavy patrols and sent out hunting parties to gather fish. When everything had been taken care of, only then did everyone crowd around Gray.

"Good to see you again!" Mari exclaimed.

"That goes double for me," added Barkley.

Snork nodded. "And triple for me!"

Striiker gave Gray a bump to the flanks in greeting. "I'm still mad you've been gone, but you sure know how to make an entrance."

"It wasn't my choice," he told everyone as he swished his tail in frustration.

"We know," Mari said quietly.

Gray didn't want to think about the information Hokuu had given him, so he caught up with Riptide Shiver matters instead. Hokuu's renegade mako finja had been harassing the mariners as well as sneaking inside their defensive screens and sending shiver sharks to the Sparkle Blue.

"They've been making us bleed for days," growled Striiker. "Those finja are some sneaky krillfaces, I tell ya." Striiker gave Shear a nod. "No offence."

"None taken," the guardian captain answered. "They are traitors with no honour."

"We weren't sure we were going to make it all the way to Fathomir," said Mari, swishing her long thresher tail pensively.

Barkley flexed his flippers. "I don't think there's any guarantee we will. Our group's too big to protect with the mariners we have left."

"Aw, come on, everyone," Snork interrupted, a little surprised at the group. "There's nothing we can't do when we swim together."

Striiker chomped his teeth together loudly. "Bark does have a point, Snork. We're spread too thinly. And every time we set a trap, they sniff it out and hit us where we're weakest."

Gray gestured to Shear with his tail. "Not any more."

The finja commander nodded, dipping his snout to Striiker. "We should be able to provide another layer of defence that Hokuu's renegades will not easily overcome."

"You guys do look really tough," commented Snork.

"But Hokuu is something else," Barkley added. "Riptide couldn't defeat him at full strength."

Gray slashed his tail back and forth. "Let's keep swimming. We have a good current at our tails. When we get to the Seazarein's territory, we'll be safe. Or at least, safer."

"That's right," said Striiker. "Maybe Takiza can grind that slimy worm into shark-bait." Striiker gestured to his subcommanders. "Once everyone has fed, we increase our speed to fifteen tail strokes a minute. Make sure the wounded keep up. No stopping until we're there." The great white looked at Gray. "Can't believe I'm rushing to get that little fish on our side."

Barkley nodded. "He's one tough betta, all right."

Gray's mind wandered. What Hokuu had revealed was beyond belief. It couldn't be true! But the mysterious betta kept so many secrets. Could Takiza have sent his father to the Sparkle Blue?

On purpose?

"Gray," said Snork. "Is something wrong? You know you can tell us anything."

Now that the sawfish had brought it up, everyone saw the worry on Gray's face. He shook his head. "I'm okay, Snork. You look like you've been through a lot, all of you do, and I'm sorry I wasn't there for you." Gray couldn't tell them these new fears yet. It wouldn't be fair to pile that on top of everything else they'd been through.

Now Gray knew how Kaleth felt. The pang of betrayal seemed to pierce his heart. In all those training sessions, Takiza had never said anything. He hoped Hokuu was lying. Even so, Gray would direct some tough questions at the betta when they got to the Seazarein's territory.

He hoped that Takiza's answers wouldn't be the ones he feared.

CHAPTER 18

"YOU CANNOT ALLOW THIS RIPTIDE SHIVER INTO our waters," Judijoan said, raising herself straight up next to the throne, the red plumes on her head arching towards it.

"I'm thinking," answered Kaleth. "You've advised, so let me think."

Kaleth had dismissed Takiza because she wanted to hear Judijoan's advice without him there. The oarfish was smarter than almost anyone she knew, but could also be a tailbender. Kaleth had wanted to swallow the betta whole by the time she'd ordered him from the throne room. To think he had known about Drinnok's treachery and hadn't shared it with her all these years!

But would I have done anything different if our places were exchanged?

Probably not. This thought troubled her.

Takiza had a point. Not even a year had passed since

Fifth Shiver's discovery of the Big Blue. Kaleth had been much more uptight and secretive with him at that time. How *could* he have known which side she was on then? How could he *not* have taken action?

Her king, Bollagan, had placed great stock in Takiza, thinking him a good and honourable dweller. Though the prehistores were more than a match for anything swimming in these waters, fins such as Takiza, Hokuu and a few others were a total surprise to Fifth Shiver because of their mysterious powers. Shar-kata had not been invented in the under-waters, although a few guardians did possess *fin'jaa* abilities. There was no need for shar-kata, because each of their ancient, prehistore species was so strong. The powers that these few fins had mastered were incredible. Had her king been afraid? Surely not.

Bollagan had felt that these waters belonged to the sharkkind and dwellers who lived here, just as the under-waters below belonged to Fifth Shiver. Yet he would not have left his fins in the darkness forever. He had wanted his subjects, and all who had been trapped below, to swim in the Big Blue, but he had been determined that they should do it in peace. Bollagan's way would have taken time and diplomacy, and Kaleth thought this was much better than causing a huge war.

This view had not been shared by Drinnok. "We should not ask for permission to swim free! If they have a problem, then let them meet us in the battle waters," was what he'd said. Drinnok had been the one who'd insisted on Hokuu being her Aquasidor after Bollagan had made it known that she would be the Seazarein, representing Fifth Shiver in the Big Blue. The king had agreed to use Hokuu as his Aquasidor to keep Drinnok on his side.

Bollagan had thought that naming a frilled shark – one rare type of sharkkind that looked the same in both the Big Blue and the under-waters – to be the link between the two oceans had been a wise decision. But not when that frilled shark was poisonously evil! What a fool she had been to agree to use Hokuu as her Aquasidor!

Luckily – and calling this luck was really stretching things – Hokuu had betrayed her before she'd had the chance to send him out on a mission as Aquasidor. Kaleth could only imagine the dissent he would have spread in this Big Blue as her representative. Since that dark day, all Kaleth's time had been spent trying destroy Hokuu and the renegade makos who had joined with him. But the wicked frill was demon hard to find, and when he was found, it was *her* guardians who died.

Was Hokuu the one who had steered Drinnok's fins in his coup? That really required no strong guidance. The brute's views had been well known to Bollagan and the Line. Graynoldus had counselled the king to watch his tail. He didn't trust Drinnok. It turned out that he had been correct. Still, Kaleth was shocked that Drinnok had betrayed his king so completely. At least Graynoldus the elder had saved his son. The families of all the others in the Line, and any allies they had, were surely swimming the Sparkle Blue. Kaleth ground her teeth, the sound making Judijoan give her a look.

"I'm still thinking," she told the oarfish.

Gray...

The son of the father she knew and respected. Gray didn't remember the elder Graynoldus, but his heart was bigger than any she had met in this watery world. A strong fin, but lacking experience. He showed promise and Takiza had trained him well, steering him from the darker currents. After his demonstration with two of her best finja, Kaleth doubted she could beat Gray in single combat.

Good thing he's on our side, she thought.

But would Gray remain in her camp if she didn't allow his former shiver the safety of her territory? Even if the fate of the entire watery world drifted in the balance?

Though the difference between them was only a few years, Gray was far less mature. Kaleth had been forced to grow into responsibility much earlier. The waters where Fifth Shiver ruled were far harsher than what they called the Big Blue. Why, she had been only a year older than Gray was now when she was named in Bollagan's Line. The under-waters could be brutal and tough. In her world, death arrived because the powerful decided it should. Was that what she wanted for these waters? It plainly wasn't what Bollagan had hoped for.

ALTBACKER

No.

She would protect the Big Blue from Hokuu and Drinnok. That had been her king's wish, and she would follow it. Besides, it wasn't in her nature to swim out and terrorize others who were weaker. She hated the fact that in her world only the strongest survived. Kaleth had to assume that only Drinnok and fins who agreed with him were in complete control of the under-waters. That would mean if they got free, there would be complete and total war.

Judijoan cleared her throat, moving her long body with the slow current that flowed through the throne cavern. "Need I remind you that our scouts say Hokuu and his renegades are attacking Riptide Shiver as they swim here? It would be lunacy to allow them anywhere near Fathomir! The chaos would provide Hokuu with the opportunity to send you to the Sparkle Blue."

"Stop being such a worry-slug. As long as my guardians protect the cavern entrance, we are safe." Kaleth gestured at the *fin'jaa* guarding the throne cavern. Even if Hokuu could get in, he wouldn't leave alive. He didn't have that much power.

But to allow him to swim close enough to try...

That was a bad idea.

And what was Velenka's role in all this? She was a mako and that didn't hover well with Kaleth. All the guardian finjas of that species had betrayed her. She didn't like makos in general since they were devious and

145

sneaky. The coup only proved it. But what was the crucial information Velenka had? Why was she important to Hokuu? Kaleth didn't know, and it was maddening.

"What if there was another way?" Judijoan asked. "One in which even Gray would be protected and we could strike at Hokuu?"

"Speak," Kaleth ordered.

"Besides you, there is only one threat that the frill must fear."

"Takiza," she said, nodding.

Judijoan waved her tail with the current. "Use the betta as bait. He did betray you, after all."

Kaleth wanted to yell at Judijoan but didn't. She held her tongue and thought it through. To do something like that was to swim a darker current than she was used to.

Of course, Graynoldus's son must be protected. The father had always been kind to Kaleth, even championing her for a position in the Fifth Shiver Line.

For now, Hokuu didn't want to harm him. But that could change.

Again Kaleth racked her brain. What was the frilled shark's plan? It followed no logic she could decipher. For some inexplicable reason she remembered the dogfish Barkley saying, "Hokuu doesn't need Velenka. There's something else going on."

Kaleth shook her head, dismissing the words of the annoying dweller. When she had to rely on advice from a dogfish, it would be time to give up the role of Seazarein.

But using Takiza to draw out Hokuu felt wrong. She was playing with his life, although the betta would certainly do the same if the situation were reversed. That much was clear from what Kaleth had learned today.

It *was* wrong and she knew that.

But . . . it could also work.

CHAPTER 19

HOKUU RIPPED INTO THE FLANK OF A LARGE
Riptide scout he had picked off. The frilled shark
motioned with his tail at the torn hammerhead. "Come!
You must be starving!"

That was true. Velenka hadn't eaten for a long while.
And the food in the Riptide prison always seemed stale.
Maybe that was because she wasn't the type of shark that
liked anyone else doing her hunting. But still, Velenka
didn't want to eat. "I caught a fat grouper earlier," she
lied.

Hokuu shook his head. He knew it was untrue but let
it pass. He had other things on his mind. "Are you ready
to tell me your ideas about getting to Gray? It would be a
shame if I had to kill a fellow prehistore. Especially one
with royal blood."

"Gray is a *royal* prehistore?" she asked. How very
interesting.

"Yes," the frill answered. "It would be good to have him alive as insurance."

"Can you tell me why letting the prehistores into this world is a good thing?" Velenka asked. "I need to explain that to Gray. Especially the part about Drinnok coming in and eating everyone. Why is it good? If I can make him understand that, maybe I can sway him."

"Maybe?" asked Hokuu, his emerald eyes narrowing to slits.

"I mean, I *will* sway him," Velenka corrected herself.

Hokuu nodded. "First of all, Tyro will be pleased. It's because of his will that I'm doing this. There's no better reason than that."

Velenka's mouth hung open. "Um, yes. But as you definitely know, we in this world don't have as good a connection with Tyro as you do."

"True, true," Hokuu said, nodding to himself.

Velenka felt her stomach clench. Hokuu believed he was doing Tyro's will by killing the sharkkind in the Big Blue. That didn't make any sense. But much of what Hokuu said to her didn't make sense. Her experience with Finnivus had been a grim and unsettling one. But at least he – and Velenka couldn't believe she was even *thinking* this – at least he wanted to rule the sharks of the Big Blue. Sure, he would eat the ones that displeased him, but for the most part, Finnivus wanted everyone to worship him.

Hokuu led her to think that Drinnok wanted the

prehistores to resettle the Big Blue and send *everyone* to the Sparkle Blue in doing it. They didn't want anyone to bow before them? It seemed odd for a royal shiver to simply want everyone *gone*.

Was Hokuu lying to her? Why?

"So when the prehistores and this Drinnok come, they'll conquer the Big Blue. And then what?" she asked.

Hokuu gracefully rose from the seabed and his kill. His eyes seemed to shine even brighter. "Oh, it'll be glorious! Drinnok and his mega-armada will sweep out of the South Sific and conquer everything in their path! And we'll get to watch!"

"I assume you'd help Drinnok rule," Velenka said, and then in a much lower voice she added, "or maybe take over if he didn't make the best decisions?"

Hokuu was on her in a fin flick, grasping her so tightly with his coils that Velenka thought she would die. "No! That's what you'd do! I know about your hunger for power. I'd never do that!" The coils wrapping her relaxed. "But I will *help* Drinnok rule, of course. You see, I'm not royalty, so according to the laws of Fifth Shiver, I can't rule."

"But Gray could . . ." Velenka whispered.

Hokuu nodded. "And so you finally get it. The Big Blue needs to be conquered by Fifth Shiver, but Bollagan the fool wouldn't even consider it. Only Drinnok saw the glory of taking our rightful place, which is everywhere."

"But if Drinnok disagrees –"

"Exactly!" said Hokuu, snapping his tail so it made a loud *crack*! "If he doesn't appreciate what I, and my species, have done ... well, there's always Gray and his claim to the throne."

"Gray won't stay still while all his friends are eaten though," Velenka said. "I know this for a fact."

The frilled shark waved his tail dismissively. "Once they're gone, what's he going to do? He'll have no choice but to follow orders or die. And if he wants to die by killing Drinnok, should that mako not give me and all frilled sharks our due, then so be it." Hokuu pointed at her. "And of course, I haven't forgotten about you. You'll also have your reward."

With dread in her stomach Velenka asked, "What is it? My reward?"

Hokuu waved his tail with a flourish. "You get to watch all this happen before you're eaten!"

"Before ... I'm eaten? How – how's that a reward?" Velenka asked in a shaky whisper.

"The reward is that you'll be eaten *last*!" Velenka could only stare as Hokuu sent ripples of excitement down the length of his body. "Think of it, you get to see the new watery world order become a reality! And then when you swim the Sparkle Blue after a bite to the gills from Drinnok himself – what an honour – *you* get to bring the news that Fifth Shiver has been fully restored ... to Tyro himself! I'm *almost* jealous of you."

"I – I never thought of it that way," Velenka told him

as her stomach heaved. By telling her this, it was as if Hokuu wanted her to swim away as fast as she could. Or betray him. That couldn't be true. Could it? "And to be clear, you won't send Gray to the Sparkle Blue. Am I right about that?"

"I'd like to have Gray as an option for later, of course. But that does depend on his actions not *forcing* me to kill him when I open the new passageway." Hokuu flicked his tail back and forth in glee and looked up towards the chop-chop. "You see? It's almost full. We're so near the appointed time. So near." He gestured at the glimmering moon far above the surface of the water. Hokuu then whispered. "And to think he was so close. If Gray had stayed where he was, he could have been a real problem."

"What does that mean?" Velenka asked.

Hokuu went back to his meal. "Never mind that. Concentrate on turning Gray to my side. You should practise what you're going to say right at the beginning since he and his friends might eat you before you can get too many words out."

Oh, right, Velenka remembered. I totally forgot I'm an escaped prisoner and they probably want to bite me in the gills. Great.

CHAPTER 20

"HALT AND APPEAR!" SHEAR CRIED, STARTLING Gray and the fins behind them. Twenty guardian finja who were hiding at the edges of the Riptide formation materialized in the water.

To the tired Riptide mariners, it seemed as if these ferocious sharkkind had appeared out of nowhere. The advance scouts screeched to a halt, bumping and jostling each other as they did so. Even though the scouts were battle-tested mariners, everyone in the armada was jumpy. And the mass of frightened shiver sharks, their pups and other dwellers in the centre were thrown into total confusion.

"Why are we stopping?" bellowed Striiker from the diamondhead position of his battle formation. "We're almost there!"

Gray was puzzled for a moment until the leader of the finja guardians dipped his snout. "Apologies, Aquasidor

Graynoldus. The Seazarein will not permit anyone but you to swim into Fathomir."

Barkley gave Shear his most wounded look. "What? No welcome feast? Are you sure?"

"I received word an hour ago as we were swimming in, so I am *quite* sure," the huge tiger shark finja replied.

"If you're not, I could go and ask," said Snork, missing the sarcasm that floated thick in the water between Shear and Barkley.

The guardian leader ignored the sawfish and waited for Gray's reaction.

"I don't much care," Gray told him.

Shear signalled with a flick of his tail and fifty massive finja appeared in the water behind him. These prehistore sharks were from Fathomir, the Seazarein's personal guard. "I'm ordered to not let any others pass."

Mari swished her tail. "Gray, maybe you shouldn't push this."

"No!" he yelled. "We're moving ahead and that's that!"

Shear didn't budge as Gray moved forward and the two sharks bumped snouts.

"You want a piece of me, Shear? It didn't work out so well for you on the training field."

The guardian captain gave Gray a pleading look. He was between sharp coral and a rough current. "Aquasidor Graynoldus, please do not do this." The big tiger didn't want to fight, but he would.

Barkley tapped him on the flank, distracting Gray as he was going to Bull Shark Rush the finja. "Are you really going to waste time brawling like a jelly-headed bully? Get in there and see what she has to say."

"Yeah," Snork said. "Let's save the fighting for that giant snake and his friends."

Mari agreed. "We're tired and hungry, anyway. And there are lots of fish here."

"With all these finja around I think we're pretty safe," Striiker added. "Go."

Gray gave Shear a cold stare. "When this is over, you and I are going to dance. But if you're still captain of the Aquasidor's guardians, stay and protect these sharkkind. That's an order."

The finja leader snapped into attention hover and dipped his snout. "Yes sir, Aquasidor Graynoldus!"

Gray turned to Barkley. "You coming?"

His friend shook his head. "That would not go down well." The dogfish motioned Gray to go on alone. "Besides, I'm hungry, too."

Gray frowned in mock seriousness. "Turtle."

"A *smart* turtle," Barkley replied. "Call me Shelley, because I'm staying put."

Gray smiled to himself. His friend had so much more confidence now that he was a subcommander and leader of the ghostfins. At least Gray had got that right. He swam towards the Seazarein's homewaters, and her fifty guardians fell into position around him. Shear was as good as his word, though. He and his twenty guardians stayed, melting into the waters, unseen once more.

Soon Gray was deep in the Fathomir homewaters and inside the even more heavily fortified throne cavern in front of the Seazarein, Judijoan the oarfish and Takiza.

Of course, everyone was displeased with him. What else is new? he thought.

"In case you were all wondering, there's peace between Icingholme and Hideg Shivers in the Arktik," Gray announced.

Judijoan shook her head at his terribly rude act. This was one of the first, and easiest, of lessons. Always let the leader of the place you were visiting, in this case the Seazarein, speak first. It was a simple rule and common courtesy.

Well, too bad!

Gray wasn't about to let Kaleth stare haughtily from her throne while making him cool his fins in silence. Not when Riptide Shiver was exposed to danger outside the Fathomir homewaters. No way! Gray set his jaw and waited for the explosion that he was sure would follow.

But there wasn't one.

The Seazarein replied in an even tone, "That's good news, Aquasidor Graynoldus. I'll want those details later. The question I'd like answered this moment, however, is why you've returned with a few more fins than when you left. Can you explain this?"

Gray switched his tail right and left. He wasn't expecting Kaleth to speak in anything less than a shouting voice. And certainly not to ask a question calmly.

"Well, yes, um – on our way here, the guardians and I detected blood in the water. When we investigated – in your name, of course – we found that it was Riptide Shiver and they were under attack by Hokuu and his renegade makos." Gray decided to make some effort to make up for his rudeness. "Knowing how much you, the Seazarein, love peace in the Big Blue, and how, um, large and good your heart is, I decided we should help them. In your name."

"So by bringing them here, you think you saved them?" she asked. Kaleth was as calm as a summer lagoon and it unnerved Gray.

"You're the most powerful shark in the Big Blue, the Seazarein Emprex of the ocean," Gray said. "I think you'll help them, because why *wouldn't* you help them?"

"You forget yourself!" shouted Judijoan as she rose perpendicular to the sea floor.

Kaleth waved off her advisor and locked eyes with Gray. "By bringing these sharkkind and dwellers, you deplete our food supplies. That makes us vulnerable to attack. As you said, we are the only force that's a match for Hokuu. *Maybe*. And only if the conditions are perfect. Your mariners are nothing compared to the mako finja, and certainly not to Hokuu. If my guardians show themselves by protecting your untrained masses, the renegades can pick them off one by one until there are none left. Then what? Who will protect your friends? By bringing these sharks to Fathomir, you have made us all less safe."

Gray swept at the sandy cavern floor with his tail. "I didn't think of that."

"No, you didn't!" Judijoan huffed.

Kaleth sighed. "But even if he had, he would have done the same thing."

Gray didn't answer. Everyone knew it was true.

"I think it is a credit to the boy," said Takiza. "Kindness and caring are never a mistake."

Gray was grateful for that. Could someone who said that actually leave his father to die? He drove the thought from his mind. This wasn't the time for that conversation.

"And if this kindness is the reason that Hokuu prevails? Will it be worth it then?" asked Judijoan. The oarfish swirled her tail through the water.

"Silence!" yelled Kaleth, slamming her tail on the ground. "I have decided."

Gray waited. He could feel that even Takiza was on edge, although the betta seemed his usual calm self.

"Your friends can stay to rest and heal." Judijoan gasped like a steam vent in the ocean floor. Kaleth gave her a baleful look and she quieted. "They stay on the far edge of Fathomir and can hunt all they want. But your mariners will be responsible for the safety of the Riptide sharks."

It was more than Gray could have hoped for. He nodded, his tail sagging as a cool wave of relief rolled down his spine. "Yes, they will."

"And one more thing," Kaleth added. "I don't want you as my Aquasidor."

Gray blurted, "What?" Takiza looked shocked, too.

"I believe you heard me," she said. "You cannot serve me *and* Riptide Shiver. Your heart is with your friends. So you are relieved of your duties until this crisis is at an end." She glanced over at Takiza. "You may also go."

The betta dipped his snout. "Please reconsider this."

"I don't believe I will," Kaleth shot back, swishing her tail from side to side. "My decision is final. Do not test me."

Takiza jerked his fins through the water and swam out of the throne room. Gray was so shocked he hovered, motionless, until Judijoan said, "That is also your signal to leave."

And so Gray swam out of Kaleth's throne room a free shark, Aquasidor no longer.

Strangely, this really bothered him.

CHAPTER 21

GRAY SWAM IN SILENCE WITH TAKIZA. NO guardians flanked them now. Gray even reached out with his senses to check if the finja were there but hidden. He felt nothing. They truly were gone.

Kaleth really meant it, thought Gray. She had Hokuu to deal with, so maybe this was the best plan. Her guardians were the best-trained sharkkind in the Big Blue. Even Finnivus's *squaline* wouldn't have stood a chance against them. Maybe Kaleth would succeed in stopping the frilled shark where Riptide had failed. Gray hoped so.

Takiza swam by his side, deep in thought. Gray waggled a fin to get his attention. "Yes? What is it now?" the betta grumped, irritated at the interruption.

"I have to talk to you about something," Gray said, taking a deep breath. "I want you to tell me the truth."

Takiza nodded. "You have earned the right. Ask what you will."

Gray decided he would start with what he knew *had* to be a lie. "Did you send one of your apprentices to the Sparkle Blue?"

Takiza became more interested and turned. "You have spoken with Hokuu. When?"

Gray shook his snout side to side. "I'm asking the questions." He went on in a softer voice, afraid of what Takiza might say. "So ... did you?"

"No," Takiza began.

"Yes! I *knew* he was lying! I knew it!" The betta sighed in an odd way that Gray found unsettling. "You didn't, right? You didn't do that. Did you?"

"I did not send my Nulo to the Sparkle Blue ... because I failed to best him in single combat."

"You what?" Gray gasped.

"It was earlier in my life," Takiza said. "I did not have the skills I possess today, so he was able to fend me off."

"That's not what I mean!" Gray said, his voice rising.

Takiza shook his thin fins. "I said I would tell you the truth. That apprentice –" The betta paused, opening and closing his mouth but saying nothing for a moment. Then, on one of the few times since Gray had known him, Takiza stumbled over his words. "That apprentice – it was ... a ... mistake to choose him. He was – not the fin I believed him to be. I did not want him to use my training for ... for ..."

"Evil?" offered Gray.

161

Takiza considered. "No, not evil. More like unpredictable havoc. I could not allow that."

"So you didn't snap his neck? You didn't kill him."

Takiza nodded, but then added, "It was not for lack of effort, though. He was very gifted. But I believe I injured him enough to make my point. He has not been seen since and probably swims the Sparkle Blue. Now, when did you meet Hokuu?"

"I'm not done with my questions," Gray said.

"I answered one of yours," Takiza told him. "I will answer your second – and last – question after you respond to mine. When did you see Hokuu?"

"On the way back from the Arktik after we'd found the Riptide sharks. I went in with Shear and the rest of the Aquasidor guardians to chase off the mako finjas and got separated. That's when I met him. My turn."

Takiza gave him a flat stare and swished his fins once for the second question. Gray stopped swimming and turned to hover. The betta did the same. "Ask," he said.

"Did you kill my father?"

Takiza didn't say anything for a moment. "That is a complex question."

Gray cut him off, whipping his tail through the water. "No, it's simple. *Did you kill my father?*"

"I must explain."

"Answer the question!" Gray yelled.

Takiza sighed and in a quiet voice said, "Yes. Through my actions, yes."

Gray had thought he would feel rage at this answer. He had been going over this possibility in his mind since he had been captured by Hokuu. But he didn't feel anger. He felt a deep sadness and found himself whispering, "No, no, no." Gray gathered himself. "Did you know he was there?"

"I did *not*," Takiza told him gently, emphasizing the word with a furious swipe of his tail. "I swear by everything I believe, Gray. As I did not know *you* were with him. I only learned that he must have been there when you came to the aid of those turtle hatchlings."

Gray's mind went back to his time with Goblin Shiver. He had gone out after patrol with a rough shark named Thrash who'd wanted to scare a turtle mother and her hatchlings. Gray had helped the hatchlings but hadn't been able to save the mother from Thrash. Takiza had done that, giving the mean tiger a comical beating in the process.

Gray nodded. The betta swam closer. "How did you fare against Hokuu? I assume you attempted to fight him?"

"Oh, I tried. And he played with me," Gray answered. "He played with me like Thrash would with a turtle hatchling. I hope you have a few tricks I've never seen, because you're going to need them."

"This is most unsettling," Takiza commented. "I was hoping his abilities had faded. Sometimes that happens with extreme age. I know this to be true."

"Shiro, I have to ask one more question."

The betta sliced his fins through the water, meaning no. "There have been enough questions for today."

"Please," Gray persisted.

The betta didn't like it but flicked a fin.

"Would you still have closed the passage if you had known we were there?"

"Yes," Takiza answered. "I would have."

"Then I guess you're no different from Kaleth." And with that Gray swam away.

He didn't see Takiza's wounded look.

SHIRO
AND
NULO

CHAPTER 22

TAKIZA WOULD HAVE LET MY FATHER DIE TO SEAL the passage between the two oceans, Gray thought. Even if he had known my father was there.

The idea boggled Gray's mind. It wasn't as if he had known his father, so his anger was muted. But he was sure Takiza would have done the same thing if it had been his mother, and that *did* bother him greatly. To sacrifice anyone's mother seemed monstrous.

When did that kind of thinking stop? What about a hundred mothers? Or a thousand pups? How about ten thousand innocent sharkkind?

But there was one thought that nagged at Gray. If you didn't sacrifice one fin to save everyone, weren't you sacrificing everyone anyway? It was easy for him to fume at the idea of someone sending his mother to swim the Sparkle Blue for *any* reason. But Takiza had to actually make the decision. He had to make that unimaginable choice. There was no good answer, was there?

Was there?

These thoughts were interrupted by shouts and the sounds of battle. On the outskirts of Fathomir, Riptide Shiver was being attacked!

Never had Gray been so glad of the chance to fight someone – *anyone* – in his life. He would stop these confusing thoughts by ramming Hokuu right in his snaky head!

Gray saw Striiker fighting like a crazy fish in the centre of a half drove of Riptide mariners. The great white leader had split his forces into groups of fifty and arranged them around the shiver sharks in a moving defensive screen. Gray liked the idea. It was more important to guard the weaker sharkkind, the pups and older fins, inside the perimeter. If Riptide's mariners were in one massed formation, the sneaky finja could evade them. This way a half drove of mariners were always within twenty tail strokes of an attack.

"Don't let them get away!" cried Striiker from the diamondhead of the small block formation.

Even though Gray could sense only ten mako finja, they were demon hard to spot. If you took your eyes off the renegades for even a fin flick, you lost where they were because of their colour-shifting ability. The finja would withdraw and stop moving for a moment, making themselves disappear to an untrained eye. Then they would rush in and take fins or strike at the gills of unsuspecting Riptide mariners. Gray used his ampullae and lateral line senses to follow their electrical shadows, which were among the brightest in the chaos.

He sped up to an attack sprint and blasted one attacker, taking his left fin cleanly and sending him spiralling towards the Sparkle Blue. Gray saw another mako lurking behind the diamondhead position. The finja increased his speed and descended on a path that would give him a shot at Striiker's dorsal fin.

"Striiker!" Gray shouted in warning. But the screams of the injured and dying, along with the sounds of battle, were too loud. Gray cut a wicked turn downwards until he nearly skimmed the seabed, then rocketed straight up in a modified Spinner Strikes attack.

I've got to get there in time! Gray thought, gritting his teeth. Water flowed past his ears with a *fwush* as he sawed his tail back and forth to gain speed. Miraculously Gray managed to find a thin path through the battle and met the finja one tail stroke before he ripped off Striiker's dorsal. He blasted the shark in the underbelly, his jaws closing tight. Blood bloomed in front of Gray's eyes and he shook the instantly dead shark out of his mouth. Striiker could only react with a startled, "Whoa!"

The great white gave him the briefest of nods before resuming his own fight. The mako finja were outnumbered and losing the battle. Gray wedged himself into Striiker's ranks, taking the place of an injured mariner in front of the diamondhead. "Get out of here," he shouted at the mariner. "You can't do any more!" There were only three mako finja left alive, and two of those were injured. Gray gestured towards their positions. "Look sharp! There, there and there!"

"Come on, you stinking muck-suckers!" Striiker bellowed. "Let's see how you do when we know where you are!" The finja would have to turn tail or be eaten alive.

That was what *should* have happened.

"It looks like you have some fight in you after all!" said an impossibly loud and cheery voice. "How about giving me a taste?" It was Hokuu, amplifying his words with his powers.

Another half drove of mariners, led by Mari with Snork, joined Striiker's group. They were harried by the vicious makos, who battled harder because Hokuu had shown himself. The frilled shark didn't feel the need to rush. He had proved he could rip through the Riptide mariners when they were at full strength. What were these few, distracted sharkkind going to do against him?

"Why not fight a worthier opponent, Hokuu?" asked an equally loud voice.

It was Takiza! The betta was arcing coloured bolts of electricity into the water and projected a glowing nimbus around himself. It was a sight to take your breath away!

It didn't impress Hokuu much. "How many times

have I told you, Nulo – never waste power in useless displays!"

The electric bolts gathered and zipped away from Takiza. They careened jaggedly through the water. The betta's control over the electricity was complete, and it divided into branches, which shocked the remaining three finja. They jerked and shuddered, then were still. The makos sank as everyone watched.

"You have said a great many things, Hokuu," Takiza answered. "Most of them untrue as well as unwise."

The frilled shark's eyes glowed with hatred. "You always were an impudent fish. Come, Taki, show me what you've learned since I was your master! Let's see if it keeps you alive!"

Off to the side and totally ignored, Striiker looked at Gray. "Should we help?"

As if in answer Hokuu launched his own vicious, forking bolt of electricity at them. Takiza deflected it before the energy roasted Gray and everyone else in the tattered Riptide formation.

"I think we stay out of the way for now," he told the Riptide leader.

"I vote with Gray," Snork agreed, his eyes wide.

Gray gestured to his friends with a fin. "But be ready. I'm going in for a closer look." He descended into the greenie using a light current to tuck himself into the kelp field. Maybe in the confusion of the fight he could get close enough to attack.

Or maybe I'll be roasted alive, Gray thought. Still, he moved forward as stealthily as he could while Striiker reorganized his mauled force.

"Come, you preening puffer fish!" shouted Hokuu. "Dip your snout into the muck and call me Shiro once more! Perhaps then I'll let you live!"

Takiza did nothing. He drifted with the current as if he didn't have a care in the world. This seriously annoyed Hokuu, and secretly Gray was overjoyed. He knew better than anyone how angry Takiza could make someone!

"Okay, if that's the way you'd like to play it!" The frilled shark swam in a twisting circle, his head meeting his tail but moving ever forward. A vivid green energy grew in the water in the centre of the circle. This ball of light was so bright that Gray had to look away.

"Catch!" said Hokuu, and the power zoomed straight at Takiza. The betta zipped to the side so fast Gray barely saw the movement.

But the energy took its own wicked turn towards Takiza's new position. If the betta was surprised, he didn't show it. Takiza again moved in a blur and stopped right in front of Hokuu. He released his own power, blasting the frilled shark, then rocketing away.

The searing energy that Hokuu had launched still trailed Takiza, though. The frilled shark yelled a strangled "Wha?" and juked away as it exploded in the water where he had been a split second before with a deep *thwooom*!

174

Hokuu faced Takiza, waving his tail from side to side in an admonishing way. "Very sneaky, Nulo. When did you become so devious?"

"I had an excellent teacher," Takiza replied.

Far from being angry at this insult, Hokuu laughed. "Oh, you!" he said. "Taki, I'm almost sorry to send you to the Sparkle Blue!" Faster than Gray's eye could follow, the frilled shark blurred and then flipped out his tail. Another sizzling bolt of energy, this one violet in colour, shot from the end of his body.

Takiza was too slow. He avoided the worst of the detonation but was buffeted by the disturbance afterwards. "You see? You'll never be my equal! You will always be Nulo!"

Then Hokuu sent four bright yellow globes of energy firing towards Takiza. These were slower than the electric ones but more powerful. The betta, noticeably slower, managed to avoid the first three. The fourth blasted a coral spire he was using for cover. The explosion shattered the coral and sent jagged pieces streaking through the water. Luckily, Takiza created a glowing shield, so he wasn't pierced by any of the razor-sharp missiles.

"Yet I am ... still here," Takiza said with some effort.

Hokuu rushed forward and stopped ten tail strokes in front of Takiza. This time he vomited a putrid liquid from his mouth. It came out in a thick, greenish stream. The vile projection melted Takiza's golden shield and it became smaller and smaller. Gray could feel the wrongness of the vomit. It was evil and would most certainly send Takiza to the Sparkle Blue if it touched him. The betta's power sputtered and began to fail.

Without thinking, Gray burst from cover. Hokuu was so intent on killing his master that the frill didn't notice until it was almost too late.

Almost.

"You!" Hokuu yelled as he jigged sideways and avoided Gray's snapping jaws. He grinned, but Hokuu was angry he had to stop his attack against Takiza. "I wondered when you were going to show up!" The frill flashed to the left but lost the betta, who took advantage of the split-second distraction to disappear. Gray did a quick roll and went after the frilled shark, who avoided him easily once again. "I don't want to hurt you, so stay out of this." Hokuu craned his snaky neck this way and that, searching for Takiza, who was nowhere to be found.

Striiker readied the Riptide mariners, drifting forward with the current. "Fins up! We're going in!"

"Let's get him!" cried Snork. Barkley, Mari and everyone in the Riptide formation were ready.

"Ganging up on me, eh?" Hokuu said, amplifying his voice again. "Nulo, where are you? Come out, come out, wherever you are!" he sang.

"He's here!" Gray said as he lunged again. "We all are!"

Hokuu yelled over his shoulder, "Okay, Taki, if you don't want to do this now, I can wait!" The frilled shark turned to Gray, then Striiker and his mariners. "I'll see you all later. Maybe in an hour, maybe a day. You won't know until it's too late!"

And with that Hokuu whooshed away so fast he left nothing but a stream of bubbles.

"At least we chased him away," Gray said.

Then Takiza was with them, shaking his head. "Hokuu left because he chose to. Nothing more."

"Why didn't you get him?" Gray asked.

"Had I attempted anything strong enough to injure Hokuu, I would have killed you," Takiza replied.

Striiker joined them along with Barkley, Mari and Snork. "So what are we supposed to do now? If we stay here and Kaleth won't help, we're going to get munched."

"Can we draw them away by moving our mariners?" Mari offered, but not too forcefully.

"Splitting up isn't a good idea," Barkley said.

The sawfish voiced everyone's worry. "What if Hokuu goes after the shiver sharks once we've gone?"

"We can't take that chance," Gray told everyone.

"He'll follow you and leave them alone," said a familiar voice, "if I come along."

Everyone turned and gasped, "Velenka!"

"SEIZE HER!" STRIIKER ORDERED. TWO RIPTIDE mariners mashed Velenka between their flanks. "Or do we just send her to the Sparkle Blue?" the big great white asked.

Velenka struggled little, moving more because she was in pain. "I'm here to help! Stop crushing me!"

Gray motioned to Striiker to let the mako speak. The great white gave a fin signal and the two mariners eased up, but hovered close to her flanks.

"Oh, come on!" Barkley groused. "Are we really going to listen to – or should I say, *believe* – anything she says? Tell me we're not that stupid!"

"We're not, right?" asked Striiker.

"No one is," said Snork, eying the mako suspiciously.

Mari nodded. "Gray, I believe in giving everyone a chance. I believe in second and third chances, even last chances. But in this case, Barkley's right."

Velenka smiled at Mari. "And here I thought we were getting to be *pals* before I was kidnapped by that prehistore maniac."

"Kidnapped! Here we go again," Barkley said, drawing his tail through the water in a circle. "Round and round. It always comes down to poor Velenka being *forced* to do all sorts of horrible things. But she's not to blame! Oh no, never that!"

"I really don't like you," Velenka told the dogfish. "Never have."

Gray gave Velenka a light slap on the flank to be quiet. The mako cringed much more than he had expected. She was definitely jumpy. Maybe that was good for them. "Velenka, we know you wouldn't be here if it wasn't in your best interests. So what are those interests?"

The mako grumbled about this but nodded. "My life. I like it. And Hokuu wants me and everyone else dead."

Mari wasn't convinced. "Gray, she lured you into a trap for Finnivus by saying this same thing. You shouldn't forget that."

It was true. Velenka had drawn him into a meeting that had ended with Gray swimming for his life. If Gray hadn't planned for her betrayal in advance, Finnivus would have had his head on a feeding platter. Velenka couldn't be trusted. But she could be counted on doing *anything* to keep herself alive. The trick was telling those two things apart. Was she here as part of some plan? That's what they had to know.

"Why did Hokuu break you out of the Riptide homewaters?" Gray asked.

The mako ground her teeth in frustration. "I don't know," she wailed. "He gave me some reasons like I was supposed to talk to you about joining him. Things I knew would never work! But it seemed like he didn't need me at all."

"I knew it!" Barkley said. "But I still don't know why he's doing that."

"Why would Hokuu follow you if you were with us?" Gray asked. "How can you be sure?"

"He promised to eat me if I betrayed him," she told everyone. "And I'm doing that right now, if you'll let me." Velenka gave Barkley a look. The dogfish forced his jaws shut before he snapped out a reply.

"Speak, then," Takiza said as he swam in front of her. His billowy fins waved back and forth in a soothing manner. "Be at peace."

Velenka snorted. "Peace. Right."

"Listen to my words," soothed Takiza. "Watch my fins as they move one way then the other. Feel the current on your flanks. How relaxing it is. Let the water whisk your worries away. You are among friends."

Velenka's usual deceiving smile fell from her face and she repeated, "Friends," in a dreamy voice. The mako's features were less guarded and, Gray thought, somehow more honest. In fact, without her expression of constant guile, Velenka was beautiful.

Barkley stared at her, open-mouthed, until he forced himself to look away. "Come on! This is dumb!" he huffed.

"No, look," Snork said, gesturing with his tail. "She's nice now. This is the shark she *hides* underneath her regular self."

Though Takiza continued to wave his gossamer fins in front of Velenka's eyes, he regarded Snork, studying him for a moment as if seeing him for the first time. Gray thought this was odd since the betta had never given the sawfish a second look before.

"Snork, you're talking crazy," whispered Striiker.

"Shh!" Mari told them in a low voice. "Watch."

Takiza's fins drifted with the current. "You will answer my questions truthfully and hold nothing back."

"I will answer truthfully," Velenka whispered, her blacker-than-black eyes gazing peacefully at Takiza.

"Why are you here?"

"If Hokuu's plan works, I'll die. I'd do anything to stop that."

Barkley nodded at Gray. "This is working, all right," he whispered.

"What are Hokuu's plans?" Takiza asked.

"To release the prehistores when the full moon rises above the chop-chop," she answered. "Fifth Shiver will conquer the Big Blue."

"That's only a few days away!" Barkley hissed. "We have no time to do anything!"

"Quiet!" Gray said, chucking his friend's jaws shut with his tail.

Takiza sighed in despair before continuing, "How will Hokuu do this?"

"I don't know."

Striiker frowned. "We're in trouble."

"*And* we don't know where we're going," Snork added.

Takiza gave Snork and Striiker a glare before turning his attention back to Velenka. "But you have an idea where to go, do you not?" prodded the betta in a relaxing voice.

"It has something to do with a place Gray has been, not so long ago," Velenka whispered. "Hokuu said Gray didn't realize how close he had been. I think that's the place where he'll release Drinnok and the prehistores."

"Rest now and do not listen to our conversation," Takiza said as Velenka hovered obediently. The betta turned to Gray. "So, where have you been?"

"The Arktik? That doesn't seem right."

Takiza shook his head. "Unlikely. The waters are too cold for the prehistores to swim into them immediately. They will need time to adjust to those temperatures. Where else?"

"You've been with me almost everywhere," he answered. "If we're counting from since we defeated Finnivus, there have been more than a few."

"Think harder, Gray," Mari told him.

Takiza pressed, "It would be a place where the barrier between the Big Blue and the under-waters were weak. A place of disturbance and chaos."

"Disturbance and chaos," Snork repeated. "Like a seaquake or something?"

"Or something!" Gray exclaimed. "The disputed lands between AuzyAuzy and Hammer Shivers. There are steam vents in the area. It's warmer there. It's near an area they call the fire waters because there are volcanoes. Could that be it?"

Takiza nodded. "It may very well be."

"All the way to the South Sific before the full moon?" Striiker asked. "That's a tailcramper of a swim. And if we're wrong..."

"It has to be the right place," Gray whispered.

"Are we absolutely sure Velenka's not lying?" asked Mari.

Snork waved his serrated bill back and forth. "Nope, she's not. Look at her." As everyone else took in the mako's serene expression, Gray saw Takiza studying Snork once more.

Barkley in particular was fascinated by Velenka's peacefulness. Or something. "Takiza, may I ask her a few questions?"

"Be my guest," the betta told him, gesturing with a fin.

Barkley swam closer. "Velenka, did you come here as a part of a plan to betray us?"

"No," she answered. "I'm afraid for my life."

"How did you escape?"

"I waited until Hokuu was fighting you. Then I sent my guard to the Sparkle Blue and hid until Hokuu left."

"Velenka, do you think your escape was too easy?" Barkley asked. Takiza raised an eyebrow to Gray, impressed with the intelligence of the question.

"No," the mako said dreamily. "There was always one guard. One finja. Nothing was different."

"She killed a finja?" Striiker mused.

Barkley waggled his tail to get their attention. "If Velenka's coming with us, I want to remind everyone what kind of fin she is."

"Barkley, you don't have to –" Gray began.

Takiza cut him off with a tail swoosh. "Watch and listen."

Barkley proceeded. "Velenka, to save your own life, would you kill me?"

"Yes," she answered.

"Would you get rid of all my friends to save yourself?"

There was no hesitation. "Yes."

"Barkley, stop it," said Mari. "We know this."

But they didn't really. And Barkley didn't stop.

"What about everyone in the Big Blue?" he asked. "Would you send *everyone* to the Sparkle Blue to save your own life?"

There was a pause. Gray grew cold inside as the

mako seemed to consider the question, even in her trance state. "I don't know."

"Why don't you know?" asked Barkley, genuinely curious.

"Because I might get lonely afterwards," the mako told them.

"Oh, my," whispered Snork, his eyes wide. "Do we really have to take her with us?"

"We'll keep her under guard." Striiker nodded, not taking his eyes off Velenka. "If Hokuu follows us because of her, he won't be attacking the rest of our shiver sharks. That's worth something."

"Since Kaleth has dumped us, it's our only option," Gray told everyone.

Barkley nodded at Takiza, signalling he was done with questioning Velenka. The betta flicked a fin between the mako's eyes. She blinked and regained her senses. She eyed everyone warily, then smiled, her needle teeth flashing. But the smile was her normal one and didn't reach her eyes, Gray noticed.

"Sorry I dozed off. Why's everyone looking at me? It's been a tough week." Velenka didn't know what was going on. "What?" she asked, edginess making her nervous grin wider. "Is this a joke?"

"I wish it was," Barkley said. He gestured at the mako with his tail. "That's who we're dealing with here, everyone. Never forget it."

Gray doubted that anyone ever would.

CHAPTER 24

GRAY FOLLOWED BEHIND THE MAIN FORCE OF Riptide sharks but ahead of the rear guard. Velenka swam in front of him, looking around warily. She thought that Hokuu or his finjas might come for her at any time. She was probably right.

He'll be coming for everyone if we're going in the right direction, Gray thought. *If* Hokuu really is planning to release the prehistores in or around the disputed waters between Hammer and AuzyAuzy Shivers. And if he isn't, we're swimming a long way for nothing.

Striiker had put Velenka under the guard of two large mariners. Gray was pretty sure that Barkley had also assigned a few ghostfins to keep an eye on her. And of course Mari didn't trust Velenka as far as she could drag the mako on to the shore. All in all, Velenka was well watched. And that was okay. You couldn't be too careful where she was concerned.

Gray saw Takiza swimming ahead of him and sped up to draw level. He didn't want to be the one who spoke first because he was still angry. But the betta swam in silence, not saying anything for five, ten, then fifteen minutes.

Oh, this is stupid, Gray thought. What am I? A pup?

He waggled his tail and Takiza looked over. "I'm still mad," he told the betta.

"That is your right," he answered.

Gray found himself grinding his teeth. "But I don't have time to be mad at you."

"Correct."

"I wasn't looking for an answer. I'm speaking here," Gray said. "When you start a conversation, then you can talk." Takiza rolled his eyes but didn't interrupt. "Everything I learned from you is useless." The betta regarded Gray with a flat stare. "I don't mean that in a disrespectful way, but all my lifting of large rocks means nothing against Hokuu. He can paralyse me with a touch and there's nothing I can do about it."

"You could *not* let him touch you," answered Takiza.

Now Gray rolled his eyes. "Wow, awesome advice! I didn't realize it was that simple. Excellent lesson, Shiro."

"Open your ears, then," Takiza said. "Training must be done in a gradual way. Do you think you could have lifted the heaviest rock I placed in your harness the first time we met?"

"Well, no. Probably not. Definitely not."

"Precisely," continued the betta. "You are at the level you are at today because of the training. That is a fact. Nothing has ever been wasted on you. You have advanced from where you began."

"Thanks, I guess," Gray told him. "But I'm nowhere near as good as Hokuu."

The betta laughed, a rare enough event that both Mari and Barkley watched for a moment before turning their eyes back to Velenka once more.

"Hokuu was my Shiro," Takiza went on. "Of course you are no match for him, everything being equal. But then, neither am I."

Gray lowered his voice. "Are you serious? If you can't take him, what are we going to do?"

"Get him to fight us when and where things are *not* equal, of course."

"And that will be when or where?"

"I do not know," Takiza answered with infuriating calm. "But when I find out, you will be among the very first I tell. And as far as Hokuu's paralysing touch or any of the other abilities he does possess..."

"Yes?" asked Gray when Takiza paused.

"You have within you the ability to counter anything he attempts," the betta answered, drawing closer. Takiza's eyes were hypnotic as he spoke, his words said with such certainty that they gave Gray a jolt of confidence. "Sometimes defeating a superior opponent is not a matter of strength, endurance, intelligence or even training. Sometimes winning against all the odds is simply a matter of will. And Gray, your will is strong. When you understand this, you can do wondrous things." Takiza paused and smiled at him. "And until then, I am here."

The betta swam off. It turned out that even though Gray felt mad, he was still very, very glad to have Takiza around.

CHAPTER 25

THEIR PACE WAS BRUTAL. RIPTIDE ARMADA HAD been terribly depleted since the destruction of their homewaters. Even with shiver shark recruits, there were fewer than five hundred fins moving towards the disputed waters near AuzyAuzy territory.

The attacks by the invisible mako finja began a day after they set out. At first the strikes were small, nibbling on the edges, causing scouts to disappear. Even though the patrols were all in force, one or two mariners would be picked off from each group and sent to the Sparkle Blue. By the time the rest had rallied, the enemy had vanished, once again invisible to the untrained eye.

Takiza was somewhere close, looking for a chance to strike at Hokuu, but Gray couldn't tell anyone. He thought that Striiker, Barkley and Mari had figured it out, but he didn't want to say the words out loud in case he was overheard. And to keep where he was a secret, Takiza couldn't give away his position by fighting a single finja when it struck. As far as the rest of the Riptide mariners were concerned, the betta had simply abandoned them.

Hokuu didn't show himself.

For now.

After they'd crossed from the North to the South Sific, the assaults became more persistent. Finja would wait for the Riptide formation to swim across their path and attack the underside or rear of the force, then break away. To counter this, Striiker changed his formation's position as they went towards their destination, never keeping a straight line. Then the renegade finja ambushed them with attacks in several places at once. The Riptide sharks were confused, trying to defend themselves from attack in every direction.

"We're being eaten alive!" Barkley said to Gray.

"Hey!" yelled Striiker as he swam past. "Stop the negative waves and do something about it!"

"What's there to do?" asked Barkley as Mari and Snork joined him. "We're a moving target. They know which way we're going and are waiting for us. Unlike Kaleth's guardians, we can't see the enemy."

Barkley had lost three ghostfins this morning and was in a foul mood. While his sharks were better than an average mariner, they gave up their advantage by swimming out in the open with the massed formation.

"It proves we're going the right way," Gray said. He tried to be confident, but it didn't quite work. They were losing sharkkind, and it was sapping the morale of everyone, including him. "We have to keep moving quickly."

"That's the hard part," Snork told everyone. "You make mistakes when you do things too fast."

Mari swished her tail as she swam alongside them. "Snork's right. What if we took some time to eat, or at least *looked* like we're taking time to eat? Then maybe we can plan a surprise for the finja."

Barkley gave the thresher an impressed nod. "I like your thinking. Gray, can we slow down? Give the ghostfins a chance to move ahead quietly and pick a spot to ambush these flippers."

"Striiker won't like it, but we could use the time to tighten up and hunt," Gray answered. "We'll still make it before the full moon."

They had made good time and were closing in on the hissing lands where Hokuu would try to release the prehistores.

Then why am I so worried? thought Gray. Striiker had sent sharks to speak with both AuzyAuzy and Hammer Shivers, but there was no sign of either. Gray realized with a heavy heart that those mariners were swimming the Sparkle Blue. Hokuu wouldn't want the forces opposing him to grow any larger. He would intercept any attempt to make contact with either of Gray's allies.

It's what I would do, Gray thought bitterly.

They had to swim the current that was flowing.

There was nothing else to do but hope they were right. A halt was called. Striiker agreed with the plan and sent out strong hunting parties. It was a good feeding area, and the mariners didn't have to swim far to bring back multiple fish so everyone could eat.

Barkley, Snork and the other ghostfins lost themselves in the greenie. There was a chance that the mako finja were waiting to pick them off, but there was also a chance the renegades had been taken by surprise when Riptide stopped and had been too far ahead to prepare. It was worth the risk.

"Forward, five strokes!" shouted Striiker from the diamondhead position in a pyramid formation after they'd eaten. The day was sunny and nice. Too nice for so many sharks to swim the Sparkle Blue.

There were attacks coming from below, so Striiker decided to move from their block shape to a pyramid with more mariners on the bottom. Any attacking makos would have to show their bellies to the Riptide mariners below them to strike the higher part of the pyramid formation.

Because Hokuu might realize Mari was missing, since he had seen her clearly during the attack on the Riptide homewaters, she had to stay. Gray swam with her, and they both kept an eye on Velenka. The mako stayed within the path the guards allowed her to swim.

"How do you think Velenka ended up, well, being Velenka?" Mari asked.

This simple question puzzled Gray. "I don't know. She couldn't have been born bad. Could she?"

Mari shook her head. "I don't think anyone is born that way."

"Do you think it could have happened to us?" Gray wondered.

The thresher's sharp intake of water caused her to sputter. "No! Never!" Gray wasn't so sure, and Mari saw this. "We've been through a lot, and we're not like her. You'd never do the things she did, and I hope I wouldn't, either."

"I've done plenty that I'm ashamed of," Gray said. "Goblin offered me a home in his shiver and I betrayed him. I mean, if you think about it."

Mari shook her head vigorously. "No, you changed sides because he wasn't a good fin," she told him. "I don't think Goblin was all evil, but his actions weren't those of a good shark. You saw that and quit. Velenka went right on being a member of his shiver until she joined up with someone even worse."

Gray nodded. When he had seen what Goblin was doing, how it was costing the lives of innocent sharkkind, he'd known he couldn't swim that current. "I also betrayed everyone in Rogue Shiver. I left you, Striiker, Barkley, Snork and Shell to go with Goblin. That's not being very good."

"Then you came and saved us," Mari reminded him. "That was good."

"But the point is I *chose* the wrong current. And I

believed I was doing the right thing. Maybe Velenka is just choosing badly."

Mari snorted. "She's done that over and over, though. How many times do you ignore it?"

"I don't know," Gray said truthfully.

"Steady," Striiker told everyone from the diamondhead, and the command was passed quietly along the ranks. They were approaching an area that was perfect for an ambush. There were towering cliffs on either side of their group, hemming them in. Swimming over the mountain range would take too much time and divert them into a current pushing in the opposite direction.

There was no telling if this was the area where Barkley had set up their counter-ambush. It would have been too risky for a ghostfin to come back and tell everyone where they were hidden, so Gray and Striiker had decided against it. Hokuu was too smart and might notice. He could even turn the ambush against Riptide somehow.

He might do that anyway, thought Gray.

Striiker looked over for a second opinion on whether they should continue between the two walls of rock. Gray nodded at the Riptide leader, and everyone advanced. The valley was long, and the jagged ranges funnelled the current so that it pushed them along at a faster pace. Gray didn't like this. Although a fast current would make the trip shorter, it also meant they would have trouble changing course if anything happened.

But soon the mountain range dropped away and the greenie below became sparse. Gray could see that no one was there. It looked like they were in the clear.

That's when the mako finja attacked from the sides and above.

All of them.

HOKUU STRIKES

CHAPTER 26

"HOLD POSITION UNTIL YOU SEE THEIR EYES!" Striiker shouted.

It was chaos.

The Riptide forces, both the scouts and main formation, were being attacked in at least twenty locations by multiple finja. There had to be at least a hundred renegades. Too late, Gray saw that the valley wasn't a good ambush site. The attackers wouldn't have any place to retreat to, even with their colour-shifting abilities. But out in the open as they were now, the renegades blended with the water. When they did strike, they were lightning quick and almost impossible to spot.

"Look out!" yelled Mari as a finja rushed Gray. But she was too far off to help. There was no time for a real defensive move, so Gray twisted to the side and whipped his massive tail round.

Whap! A solid hit!

Solid, but lucky. I'll take it, thought Gray.

A Riptide mariner struck the finja, and it spiralled towards the greenie, streaming blood. Many other attacks were succeeding, though. Riptide sharks screamed in agony as they swam the Sparkle Blue. Gray saved one hammerhead mariner from a finja by ramming the attacker in the gills. That mako managed to retreat, but it wouldn't be fighting again today.

Striiker's mariners had compressed their position to defend themselves, with even the scouts and the defensive screen joining his pyramid formation. The finja sensed victory and pressed their assault.

It was a mistake. Their first one.

And it couldn't have come at a better time.

From their well-concealed positions, Barkley, Snork and the rest of the ghostfins launched straight up, each doing a classic Spinner Strikes move. And from this angle they could see the renegades clearly! Viewed from underneath (against the backdrop of the sun-lightened chop-chop) the finja weren't invisible: they were dark blue blotches against the lighter blue water.

And even better, the makos didn't expect an attack from below.

Blood bloomed in the ocean around the besieged Riptide formation. And this time, it was the blood of mako finja! Part of the plan was to give each one a bite, even if an underside ram would be more effective. That way, the renegades would leak blood. And because of that, they weren't invisible to the main force of Riptide mariners any more.

"Attack!" commanded Striiker. "Let's show these chowderheads who we are!"

"*RIPTIIIIDE!*" came the thundering response as sharkkind roared out in all directions wherever a stream of enemy blood was spotted. It was the biggest loss ever inflicted on the dangerous finja. Riptide had finally succeeded in challenging the renegades to a massed fight and it was going their way!

"Oh-ho-ho!" came a sprightly and impossibly loud voice that chilled Gray's blood. "That was very sneaky! Retreat, my finja!"

Hokuu appeared, swimming in a circle and creating a whirling vortex that scattered the Riptide mariners nearest him. The remaining prehistore makos raced past the frill and into the seething waters ahead. During the battle, the current had pushed everyone to the edge of the disputed lands, where Hokuu had been hiding all along.

They had guessed correctly after all.

Suddenly Shear and fifty guardians struck. It was only Hokuu's lightning-fast reaction, which blasted them away with a powerful ball of energy, that saved him.

Gray rejoiced. Shear was here! That meant that Kaleth *had* sent her guardians! Deep down, she wasn't hard-hearted!

"Joining the party, too, eh? Well, you may have all

found your way here, but there's nothing you can do to stop me!" Hokuu screamed. With a wave of his tail, a shimmering barrier appeared, walling off the ocean ahead of Gray and everyone else. "You may as well swim back the way you came!"

Shear skidded to a halt by Gray. "We must get through! This may be our only chance to face Hokuu with the complete guardian force!"

"Then let's get him!" cried Striiker. He raced towards the barrier and smashed into it as hard as he could. The wall stopped him cold as if he'd rammed a thousand-year-old coral pillar. Gray went over to the great white, who shook his head woozily. "I'm still kind of stupid sometimes."

"No, it's a good idea! But we need to do it differently," Gray said. "Shear, everyone! Push!"

Mari helped Striiker order their mariners into lines so they wouldn't jostle each other. Shear and his guardians took the centre. "Set!" shouted Gray. The Riptide and guardian sharkkind put their snouts against the hazy surface of the barrier. Even though it looked like a thin line of cloudy water, it was cold and hard. "Swim! Swim forward!"

For a full thirty seconds the wall did not budge despite the massed power of over five hundred sharkkind and guardians. Hokuu waved his tail at them from the other side, his horrible smile growing even wider. "Silly sharks! You look so stupid!"

"I'll show you stupid!" shouted Striiker.

Hokuu swam in front of the great white on the other side of the barrier. "You already have – by being here! *Ohh*, you really set yourself up for that one!"

"Concentrate! Keep swimming!" shouted Gray.

The barrier began to bend and everyone inched forward. But it was painfully slow. Gray's body ached from the effort. "Come on, do it!" he urged everyone.

"It's moving!" exclaimed Snork.

Hokuu's snaky tail twitched. "Stop this! You'll never get through, so why try?"

"PUSH!" Gray countered. Sharkkind around him gasped and strained but the barrier curved noticeably.

"No, no, no!" cried the frilled shark. "You'll ruin everything!"

With a hissing *riiiip*, the barrier gave way and a huge hole was torn through it. Shear and his guardians were quickest and they whipped through the waters after Hokuu with Gray and the Riptide mariners following. The frilled shark easily kept ahead of everyone chasing him.

"Oh no!" wailed Hokuu, his eyes wild and rolling. "How could you break through my shield!" The frilled shark darted into hissing waters. Everything was clouded by the sulphur and whatever else was being vented from the sea floor.

"After him!" yelled Striiker. "No mercy!" The Riptide sharks got into formation and followed.

205

Gray saw the frilled shark heading towards a single column of smoke that glowed red on the sea floor. Lava! That had to be where the walls between the two oceans were thinnest!

Hokuu was leading them right to it!

The frilled shark flashed ahead. His amplified voice screamed, "You'll never stop me from freeing Fifth Shiver! I'll do it right now!"

Gray sped after Hokuu, but something worried him.

The full moon *hadn't* risen yet.

In fact, the sun was only now going down. And why was Hokuu so vocal about what he was going to do, unless . . .

Unless this was a trick.

Or a trap!

"SHEAR, STOP!"

But Shear and the guardians were too far ahead to hear anything. Gray wheeled as fast as he could, but the advance guard from Riptide streamed past him.

"STOP! STOP!" he yelled as the pyramid formation of mariners came forward.

"What are you doing?" yelled Striiker from the diamondhead. The main force of Riptide mariners was a little slower than the advance guard.

"IT'S A TRAP!" Gray yelled. He made sure that Mari, Barkley and Snork heard.

"EMERGENCY STOP!" bellowed Striiker. The racket of the hissing waters carried his words away. Luckily,

Olph the battle dolph was there. Learning dolphin click-razz language was now compulsory for every Riptide mariner. The clicks, whistles and razzes cut through even the noisiest of waters. Olph pierced the chaos with Striiker's command.

Sharks piled into one another! It definitely wasn't the smoothest of emergency stops, but it got the job done. The water was thick and cloudy, the taste of sulphur choking everyone. Gray's eyes watered as he looked for Hokuu. It was a confused mess!

But stopping saved their lives.

"Who wants boiled shark?" yelled the frilled shark, hovering on the other side of the largest of the hissing vents. With a wave of his tail he sent a bolt of energy into it. The power burst activated the lava gurgling under the seabed.

FWHOOOOM!

There was a thunderous roar and an explosion of sizzling lava that created a gaping hole in the seabed a half kilometre around! The burst of hot gas burned almost every guardian and Riptide advance sharkkind above it to black ash. What was left of them was blown apart by the roiling updraught of water that came afterwards.

The lethally hot water would reach Gray and his friends in less than a second. And inside the explosion was lava rock, solidified into jagged spikes by the colder sea and hurtling towards them. Gray could do nothing but close his eyes and wait to be pierced by the shards with everyone else.

But it didn't happen.

Instead, the boiling water stopped a metre from Gray's snout. It whooshed upwards as the lava spikes clattered against an invisible barrier. Wait, it wasn't invisible. It was hard to see because the water itself was so murky and thick.

This was Takiza's doing.

Gray spotted the betta, rigid from the effort as he fed his power into a bright bluish shield that protected everyone. When the worst of the explosion was over, Takiza allowed the barrier to dissolve.

"I hate you, Taki! Do you know how long that trap took to set up? DO YOU?" screamed Hokuu from the other side of the crater. The lava inside had solidified in the colder water rushing on to it.

Steam gurgled and hissed all around them, but the frilled shark amplified his voice so everyone could hear. He was angry this time. *Really* angry. Not like before, when he had been acting, which was obvious to Gray only in hindsight.

Now Hokuu was furious and his glittering eyes blazed with hate. "You have spoiled my fun for the last time. This is the end, Taki. Now ... YOU DIE!"

CHAPTER 27

SHEAR AND A FEW OF THE OTHER GUARDIAN finja had miraculously survived, but had been rolled and tumbled in the violent waters, and badly injured. Gray had no idea how anyone near the explosion had survived. The vast majority were simply gone.

Hokuu jittered through the water, supple as a piece of greenie in a twisting current. His turns were so sharp and unpredictable it was hard to follow his blurred course with the naked eye as he stabbed mariners through the gills with his pointed tail or bit their fins, tails, or heads off. All the while the frilled shark raced towards Takiza and Gray. Striiker and the other Riptide mariners were no help, being tossed about by the remains of the tremendous explosion of lava that Hokuu had almost lured them into.

Almost, had it not been for Takiza. The betta had saved them once again.

Hokuu came to a halt ten tail strokes away and launched a jagged bolt of lightning which brightened the water as it flashed forward. Takiza fluttered his gauzy fins and Gray was shoved sideways by a turbulent force created by his power. "Flee, you fool!" the betta commanded as he blocked the lightning bolt with one of his own.

Gray swam at Hokuu, but the frilled shark dodged and gave him a paralysing touch. Gray couldn't move a muscle and drifted towards the seabed.

"Taki, I will deal with your apprentice after I kill you!" Hokuu yelled, anger making his green eyes glow.

"Must you always bleat like a whiny sea cow?" replied Takiza. "It is ever so tiresome." The betta seemed composed, but the mighty forces he'd summoned in the battle so far had taken a fierce toll. He was in a fight for his life.

And there was nothing Gray could do to help!

Hokuu and Takiza exchanged jolts through their mastery of shar-kata. There were explosions and blistering thumps of power. Both had to retreat from the other during the fight, but Gray saw that Takiza was getting the worst of it.

Hokuu kept advancing, coming closer and closer. He launched his attacks from ten strokes away, then five, then only two. This put Hokuu in range to use his fierce, spiked tail. It whipped through the water, creating a high-pitched whine as the frill tried to slice

Takiza in two. The betta bounced and darted, somehow avoiding the strikes, but it was all he could do to stay alive.

Gray felt helpless as he struggled against the paralysis. The tide had pushed him on to a thick clump of brown greenie, rough against his belly. It can't end this way, he thought. Striiker and the mariners were still getting their fins underneath themselves and couldn't help.

It's up to me, Gray thought.

He strained to move. The more he struggled, the more his muscles didn't want to work. Then he remembered Takiza's words about will. Maybe it wasn't about physical effort at all.

Gray concentrated. He imagined his tail swishing back and forth – and it did! But it was only the tiniest of flicks. He must do better!

"I have you now!" Hokuu's tail split the water in a blur and struck Takiza's shield, smashing through it and sending the betta tumbling. The frilled shark reversed position, batted the betta the other way, and then paralysed him. "So now it ends, Taki. Do you have any last words?" Hokuu's pointed tail poked Takiza gently on the forehead.

"What is the point of speaking with one who will not change his mind?" asked Takiza with a calm that infuriated Hokuu.

"I hate when you answer a question with a question! You always had such a high opinion of yourself!" huffed the frilled shark. "Even when you were my Nulo, you fancied yourself as master. Didn't you, you arrogant little puffer fish?"

"You say this," answered Takiza. "So it must be true."

Gray closed his eyes and cleared his mind as Hokuu smacked Takiza from side to side with his tail, toying with him.

There was still time.

Gray blocked out everything and pictured the warm, calm waters of the Caribbi. He could swim as fast as he wanted. He just knew he could. There was nothing to stop him. His tail swished easily in his imagination. When Gray opened his eyes, he would be moving.

And he was. He hurtled at Hokuu as the frilled shark drew his spine-sharp tail backwards for the killing blow.

"Enough of your nonsense!" Hokuu spat. "Time for you to go!" The frilled shark's tail zipped towards Takiza –

But Gray blasted into Hokuu from his blind side. The point of the frill's tail grazed the side of Takiza's face. Gray raked Hokuu's flank with his own dagger teeth.

"YOU!" Hokuu screamed. "IMPOSSIBLE!"

A sizzling bolt of electricity flashed past Gray and struck the frilled shark, causing him to shudder violently until he swept the energy away.

Hokuu looked at Takiza, who was listing to the side as he hovered. "It doesn't matter, fools. I've done what I wanted to do. And we *will* meet again!"

"Stop him!" shouted Takiza as he loosed another burst of energy. But this one was weak and didn't even reach Hokuu. Gray rushed the frilled shark, but he disappeared in a streak of bubbles.

"Are you okay?" Mari asked Gray.

"I'm all right. But Takiza's been hurt!"

The betta waved his fins dismissively. "It is no matter. I must go."

Striiker joined them. He had a gash on his side that was leaking blood, but it didn't look too bad. "Thanks for saving our lunch, Takiza, but where are you in such a rush to go?"

"Fifth Shiver isn't coming to the Big Blue today," Gray told the Riptide leader. "The full moon meant nothing! The whole thing was a fake, like Barkley said."

"Oh, really?" Striiker asked pointedly as he eyed Velenka, who had been hiding deep in the greenie. She heard, though.

"I didn't know about that!" she cried. "I swear it!"

"We'll see about that when we put you in a cell with a thousand hungry cuttlefish!" the great white told her.

"NO!" Velenka began to weep. "I didn't know!"

"I don't think she did," Snork said.

Takiza snapped his gauzy tail and it made a cracking noise, quieting everyone. "She was merely a pawn. Hokuu allowed Velenka to escape to give us the information that would lead to this trap."

"Right, to get us here and boil us alive," said Mari.

213

"Not us! We were only a bonus," said Barkley. The dogfish motioned to the injured Shear.

Gray couldn't believe he had been so dumb not to see any of this! "It was for Shear and the guardians," he told everyone. "Kaleth's defenceless!"

Shear joined them. The captain of the guardians could barely swim and was horribly burned on one flank. He had avoided the blast of super-heated lava by the thinnest of margins. "I must go. The Seazarein ordered ... almost all of us here ..." The tiger shark finja lost consciousness.

Gray grew cold. Kaleth was left with only a few guardians and Hokuu was roaring towards her. He would get inside Fathomir this time because no one was there to stop him. Everyone was too far away to do anything about it!

CHAPTER 28

"LET'S FORM UP!" STRIIKER COMMANDED. "WE'VE got a triple-time swim to the North Sific ahead of us!"

Riptide's subcommanders relayed the great white's orders. Though all the mariners took their positions quickly, every one was exhausted from the long journey and ferocious fighting they had been through.

Mari tapped the Riptide leader's flank with her long-lobed thresher tail. "Striiker, they're too tired. There's no way."

"No one's tired!" Striiker yelled. He listed to the right and winced from his own injury. "We'll just have to suck it up," he said in a weakening voice.

"It'll be tough, but we should try," added Snork.

"You will never make it to Fathomir in time," Takiza told them. "I will go."

Gray sized up the betta. His energy seemed low. The effort of saving the Riptide armada and his battle with

Hokuu had taken its toll. "You can't, Shiro. You'll kill yourself."

"All fins must one day swim the Sparkle Blue. Perhaps today is my day."

Barkley swished his tail. "You've fought Hokuu twice and both times got the tail end of it. What makes you think you can win even if you get there in time?"

Takiza gave the dogfish a smirk. "I have heard that the third time is always a charm." He gestured at everyone gathered. "If you would all be so kind as to move . . ."

Gray stuck his tail in front of Takiza before he could zoom away. "Wait, Shiro. Let me do it."

"Bah!" Takiza grumbled. "You are not ready."

Gray swam in front of the betta and looked him straight in the eyes. "I say I am ready. Now show me what to do."

Takiza held Gray's stare. After a moment, he nodded. "Perhaps you can be of use."

"What do you mean?" asked Snork. "Are you going to magic yourselves over there?"

Gray cut Takiza off before he could call the sawfish a dumb sea cow or something worse. "Shar-kata isn't magic, Snork. It's a form of specialized training which allows you to gather the power of the sea and turn it into things like energy bolts. It can also help you swim very fast."

"I must go with you," Shear said. Being a captain of

the guardians, the big tiger was intent on defending the Seazarein. But Shear had been scalded so badly the skin on his right flank was cracked and black. Any exertion would probably kill him.

"Us too," Barkley added, gesturing at Striiker, Mari and Snork.

Takiza swooshed his fins, shaking his head for added emphasis. "None of you are coming!" he announced. "It would send every one of us to the Sparkle Blue. I must go with Gray and attempt to prevent his stomach from exploding or his eyes boiling from their sockets should he make a mistake."

"Oh . . . gross," Snork said in a quiet voice.

Gray tried to keep his most confident look on his face. He hadn't known there could be such a bad effect. I sure hope I don't explode, he thought.

"Come," Takiza told him. "I will begin, then you will take over, for I do not have the strength."

"Shiro," Gray began, very worried.

"You will not explode," the betta said quietly. "But it is your first time attempting this. You will not have the ability to bring others with you, especially because you are such a large fish."

"Mum says I'm big-cartilaged," Gray interrupted, trying to get a grin from Takiza.

The betta shook his head. "I am glad that you are in such good spirits. But this is dangerous, Gray. Clear your mind and observe the energies I call forth. See them, not with your eyes but with your other senses. We will have only one chance."

Gray nodded. "I'm ready."

"We shall know soon if that is the truth," Takiza replied, hovering over Gray's snout between his eyes. He began waving his gauzy fins rhythmically. "Let your senses expand outwards, touching everything around you."

Gray did so. He had grown much better at this and could identify the electrical shadows of all his friends. He sensed the hundreds of Riptide mariners nearby and even their injuries. He could feel the many different dwellers in the greenie, rocks and coral below.

"Sense the power inside the tides themselves. Gaze into the water and finally see, Gray. Look deep and understand. Only then can you draw strength from the ocean's beating heart."

For a moment Gray couldn't feel anything, but then there was ... something.

There was a slight haziness, but not from the sulphur and silt in the water.

This haze glowed.

It wasn't caused by any lumo or reflection. This infused the waters all around them. When he breathed, this glow became part of him, giving energy in addition to the oxygen in the water. Gray looked deeper, but not with his eyes. He *felt* the energy and saw that it was coming from millions and millions of tiny sparkles.

Countless, everywhere and all around! Some glowed brightly, others stuttered and disappeared, new ones taking their place in an endless cycle. Gray's heart leapt from the simplicity and beauty that he had never known was all around him and everyone else living in the Big Blue.

"I see it!" Gray whispered. "I can see it now. It's ... beautiful."

"Draw the energy inside yourself," Takiza told him.

Gray concentrated on pulling the sparkles – there were so many! – into himself. But the more he tried, the further the dancing shimmers moved away.

"You must not force the energy. Do not command," Takiza soothed. "Instead, ask politely."

Gray opened himself, inviting the energy his way. Slowly the flitting motes drifted towards him. The sparks didn't go into his mouth like Gray thought they would. Instead, they merged with him wherever they touched his body. Gray began to feel giddy and excited.

"Good," Takiza whispered. "Control your emotions. Take what the waters give you and swim slowly as if hovering against a light current."

Gray waved his tail back and forth.

It shouldn't have moved him forward at all, really.

But it did.

Gray shot forward as fast he had ever swum in his life. "YEE-HAA!" he shouted in joy. "I'm doing it! I-am-doing-it!" The ground below blurred into a continuous green-and-brown ribbon. "It's incredible! It's amazing! It's – *WHOA!*"

Gray's words caught in his throat as the mountainside of the valley that he and the Riptide mariners had swum past appeared out of nowhere! If Takiza hadn't somehow moved them twenty tail strokes to the left, they would have splattered themselves against the rocks. Gray concentrated on keeping a straight line with blue water ahead.

When they were moving smoothly, Takiza tapped him on the snout. The betta had no trouble staying there, of course. "Avoid smashing into things at this speed, Gray. It would be *unwise.*"

"Yes, Shiro," he answered, a little embarrassed.

Gray could feel the power in the ocean and all the living things they sped past. The glowing sparkles anticipated his path and moved so that they would enter his body as he passed. They gave him so much energy it was almost too much to bear.

"Slow down, we are approaching the Seazarein homewaters," Takiza told him.

Gray reduced his tail strokes until the ground below moved at less than a blur. Fewer of the glowing sparks crossed his path. Then with a *pop!* Gray was swimming normally again. But he didn't feel tired at all. He felt refreshed!

They were only a short swim from the entrance of Kaleth's throne cavern. The Seazarein's homewaters were still and quiet. "There is blood in the water," Takiza said in a low voice. "Quickly, inside!"

Gray swam swiftly, readying himself to battle Hokuu. Takiza detached himself from his snout and flashed forward, using his own powers. Gray tried to do fast swim but found he couldn't. Maybe he *was* tired. Maybe Takiza was the only reason Gray had been successful. He didn't know. The betta disappeared into the cave first and Gray followed. The smell of blood was thicker there. He accelerated, bursting into the cave, shouting, "*AHHHH!*" to scare Hokuu if he was waiting.

But the frilled shark wasn't there.

Gray retched. Ten of the Seazarein's guardians, once so fearsome, were ripped and torn. They floated and tumbled in the light current of the royal cavern, all swimming the Sparkle Blue. And lying across her throne was Kaleth. A series of jagged bites had been taken from her body, with a deeper one on her gills.

Judijoan was by her side. The oarfish bent her neck and faced Gray and Takiza. "You did this," she accused. "Because of you, the Seazarein is dead!"

CHAPTER 29

GRAY STARED, DUMBFOUNDED, AT THE Seazarein's torn body lying across her throne. Takiza hung his head as Judijoan scowled. "This is on your heads."

Then Kaleth stirred.

"Old friend," she said in a breathy whisper. "Hokuu did this and no one else. It's not right to blame them."

"You're alive!" Judijoan gestured at Gray with the tail of her long body. "Don't hover there like a lumpfish! Find the doctor and surgeonfish!"

Before Gray could streak out of the cave, Kaleth called out in a surprisingly strong voice. "Stop! It's no use, Judijoan. I will swim the Sparkle Blue soon."

"No!" cried the oarfish, stuttering ripples flowing along her long body.

Kaleth weakly curled her tail, motioning Gray and Takiza forward. "Come closer. We must speak before I leave these waters."

The betta bobbed his snout lower than Gray had ever seen. "I apologize for having deceived you. I ask your forgiveness."

Kaleth nodded. "Of course. And I understand why you did what you did."

Gray dipped his snout also. "Kaleth, I'm sorry if I made you mad by failing so many times. I tried my best. And thank you so much for sending your guardians to protect us."

Kaleth smiled regretfully. "Gray, I did not send my guardians to protect you, but to use Takiza as bait to draw Hokuu out from hiding."

"An admirable idea," Takiza said.

The Seazarein wiggled her injured body. "As you can see, it didn't work as I had hoped. Hokuu was always two tail strokes ahead of me."

Gray was shocked by this confession. Kaleth patted his flank with her ruined tail.

"I know I've disappointed you with this action, Gray. When you're making the decisions, remember that sometimes distasteful things have to be done for the good of all. Sometimes you will be forced to be the bad fin." Kaleth coughed, releasing a cloud of blood as she did so. "And tell Barkley I apologize. If I had listened to him, perhaps I would not have landed in Hokuu's trap. Your friend has the wits and heart of a megalodon."

"He'll be pleased to hear that, and sorry about this. And I'll try and understand what you, and even Takiza,

223

have done," Gray told them. "I know you're both good fish at heart, even though you've done bad things. I'm happy to not have to face those kinds of decisions."

"But you will, Gray," Kaleth wheezed. "*You* are the Seazarein now."

And then Kaleth's gills stopped moving, and she swam the Sparkle Blue.

A few days later, Gray glided down towards the Seazarein's throne, carving a path between his friends and the remaining guardians who watched from either side. Judijoan said the words that would make him Seazarein, but Gray hardly heard them. He had barely been a passable Aquasidor and now he was being promoted to Seazarein Emprex, ruler of the entire Big Blue.

This is crazy, he thought.

He hoped against hope that Kaleth would come out from a hiding place, alive and well, and Takiza would say something like, "Did you actually think we were serious?" even though he wouldn't say it like that. There would be bigger words and more insults. But Takiza didn't speak.

Instead, his master dipped his snout to Gray as he passed.

Then everyone did!

Has the entire Big Blue gone mad? Gray thought for the hundredth time.

He reached the end of the hall and the ramped area before the throne. Judijoan hovered straight up and down in the water, towering over everyone. "Bow before Tyro and all the Big Blue," she commanded, and Gray did so. "Arise now, Seazarein Emprex of all the waters, emperor of the seven seas and magister guardian of the Big Blue."

Gray turned as everyone chanted, "Hail! Hail! Hail!"

Judijoan whispered, "It's customary to say a few words."

"About what?" he asked the oarfish.

"About anything you think is proper. After all, you *are* Seazarein Emprex," she answered in a low, exasperated tone. "Act like one."

"Right," Gray mumbled.

Everyone in the cavern waited. He could see the strain on their faces. Shear and his guardians numbered barely twenty now, and all were injured. That used to be the size of the Aquasidor's guard. Takiza was as unreadable as ever, but somehow he seemed older and more frail. Gray's friends from Riptide Shiver were there: Barkley, Mari, Striiker and Snork. They'd been beaten down by the destruction of their homewaters and everything else they had been through. At least Snork mustered a hopeful smile and flicked his tail in support. Other than that there was a pall hovering over the cavern, a sense of bleak hopelessness.

They had no clue when Hokuu would set his plan

into action to release the prehistores. The frill had fooled them so thoroughly with the trap he'd set it was foolish to think they could figure out where this would really happen. It felt like they were living on borrowed time.

Gray cleared his throat. "It's been a very tough month. Here we are, so soon after one threat, facing something even worse. Those of you who know me understand I'd gladly find a quiet reef and live out my days in peace. But that isn't the current we're in today. The current we swim is a dark one, full of danger and sorrow. Though we're fewer than we'd like, it's up to us to stop Hokuu. I know, Riptide has already been destroyed, so what's the point? Because it's not just our Big Blue that's threatened, but everyone's."

Gray swished his tail as he looked over the sharkkind gathered in the cavern. "There will be many sharks and dwellers in the far reaches of the oceans who won't even know what we are doing. They won't know how much they owe to you brave few. But I do and I thank you for it from the bottom of my heart. I could never manage it by myself and I'm thankful you're here with me. I promise never to ask anything of you that I wouldn't do myself. And on the day we meet Hokuu and his allies in the battle waters, I'll be there, swimming the diamondhead."

Gray drifted down the ceremonial pathway, stopping in front of Barkley. "Will you swim with me, Bark?" he asked his friend.

"You know I will," the dogfish answered, giving Gray a tap to the flank.

"And you, Mari?" She nodded, unable to say the words.

"I am so there!" Striiker yelled, not waiting to be asked.

"Don't forget me!" Snork added.

Shear moved forward. He hadn't been thrilled when he'd heard that Gray would be Seazarein. Not by a long shot. Now he dipped his snout. "The guardians are with you."

Gray looked to Takiza. The betta nodded before saying, "And I will be at your side also ... even when you do not wish it."

This caused a ripple of laughter in the cavern. It was a welcome sound, and soon everyone was thumping him on the flank. It was wonderful.

But in the back of his mind Gray wondered ... just where was Hokuu?

And what would he do next?

EPILOGUE

THE FIRE WATERS WERE GLORIOUSLY HOT, almost boiling. The sea here was black from the sulphur and rich earth that came hissing from the steam and lava vents. The seabed below glowed in places, orange light shining through the murk before it was snuffed out in a sizzle or, better yet, an explosion of jagged lava chunks. Hokuu could feel the pulsating pools of hot lava just below the surface, waiting, waiting to thunder into the ocean.

This was where it would begin.

This was where the new watery world order would take hold.

The Seazarein was dead!

Hokuu knew the soft-hearted fool would never allow Gray to be without protection, no matter what she told everyone else. And most of Kaleth's guardians had also gone up in a flash of glorious heat.

How sweet was that?

Very sweet indeed.

But it would have been even better if he had been able to send his bothersome ex-apprentice, Takiza, to the Sparkle Blue. Gray had somehow overcome Hokuu's considerable power and broken free at the absolute worst time, saving his irritating master from certain death!

Could Gray have been faking the first time they fought and not used all his shar-kata powers?

No, the boy wasn't that smart. He couldn't be. It was only dumb luck taking the form of a fat pup.

Hokuu would finish Takiza and gain control of Gray. Failing that, though, he would send the meddling megalodon to the Sparkle Blue to be with his father. Drinnok would want him done away with in any case. Drinnok would storm into this world like a flashnboomer and all would bow before him before being swept away.

It would start here, in these fire waters.

Not yet.

But soon.

A giant geyser of lava erupted from the seabed five tail strokes to his right and Hokuu was almost burned to a crisp. That was fine. Sometimes you got a little singed when you swam the fire waters.

Hokuu wouldn't have it any other way.

It will be glorious, he thought.

Acknowledgements

First I'd like to thank Ben Schrank, president and publisher of Razorbill, who took a huge chance in letting a first-time author write this series.

Also in the Penguin family, thanks to Emily Romero, Erin Dempsey, Scottie Bowditch, Courtney Wood, Lisa Kelly, Anna Jarzab, Mia Garcia, Tarah Theoret, Shanta Newlin, Bernadette Cruz, and everyone else from marketing, publicity and sales. My hardworking design and production team: Vivian Kirklin in managing editorial, Kristin Smith in design and Amy White in production. And special thanks to Laura Arnold, my fantastic editor and fin-tastic conspirator on all things Shark Wars.

I'd also like to thank Wil Monte and his talented crew at Millipede Creative Development, led by Jason Rawlings, for creating the Shark Wars game app. I hope to one day meet you lot in Melbourne for a pint. Thanks to illustrator Martin Ansin for the Shark Wars covers and endpapers, which look better than I could have ever imagined; and of course my agent Ken Wright at Writers House for all his hard work.

To my good friend Jim Krieg, who has done so much that I can never repay him, although I will certainly try. And finally to my family and friends who were so supportive through the years. Best wishes to you all.

ERNEST JOHN ALTBACKER is a screenwriter who has worked on television shows including *Green Lantern: The Animated Series*, *Ben 10*, *Mucha Lucha* and *Spider-Man*. He lives in Hermosa Beach, California.

Visit **www.SharkWarsSeries.com** to learn more and to play the Shark Wars game!

Bright and shiny and sizzling with fun stuff . . .

puffin.co.uk

WEB FUN

UNIQUE and exclusive digital content!
Podcasts, photos, Q&A, Day in the Life of, interviews
and much more, from Eoin Colfer, Cathy Cassidy,
Allan Ahlberg and Meg Rosoff to Lynley Dodd!

WEB NEWS

The **Puffin Blog** is packed with posts and photos from
Puffin HQ and special guest bloggers. You can also sign up
to our monthly newsletter **Puffin Beak Speak**

WEB CHAT

Discover something new EVERY month –
books, competitions and treats galore

WEBBED FEET

(Puffins have funny little feet and
brightly coloured beaks)

Point your mouse our way today!